ENOUGH! NOW NO MORE

MADHUSRI K.

First Edition : Year 2024

ISBN : 9798894757308

*

All Rights Reserved with : Madhusri K. (Madhu Shrivastav)

*

Editor : Ganvru Pramod

*

*

Publisher : Notion Press Media Pvt Ltd,
#7, Red Cross Road,
Egmore, Chennai, Tamil Nadu 600008

Email IDs: publish@notionpress.com, sales@notionpress.com,
editor@notionpress.com

Phone Number: +91 44 46315631

Contents

Foreword

Story is a popular genre of Hindi writing which is a mirror of the society as well as the mirror of particular period. If we take a glance at the development journey of story-writing, the story of every period is influenced by the environment of its time. Human sensitivity does the work of connecting the ideological and cultural differences of a time-period. The excitement of the storyteller's or storywriter's senses determines the direction of the story and the excitement, that arises in the heart, takes the form of a story through long or short expression.

In our society where we live, every day some story passes before our eyes. We can know it only when we are living with sensory awareness, and provided that our subtle vision can see it.

The entanglement in the debate of our thoughts and the distraction of the mind from the events around us gives the basis of story-writing to us. Our sensitive experience arising from our gross environmental attachments often becomes inner suffocation. Due to this inner suffocation, we feel helpless; and due to this we also feel struggleful. Ultimately this struggle gives edge to our writing.

In true sense, the credit for the creation of the story goes to our inner turmoil. This turmoil does not allow us to rest in peace until it finds a way out.

My stories are woven on many ideological values like social discrepancies spread all around, women's identity and man's sense of ego. In other words, they stand on the emotional ground of burning topics. Careful readers can tell how successful these stories are in their objectives.

••••••

Madhusri K.

Preface

Exordium about the book : 'Enough! Now No More'

The book 'बस! अब और नहीं' (Enough! Now No More) is originally wiritten in Hindi by reknowned poetess / prose writer Madhushri K. In my view, this book is one of the best creations of the prose-world. I, being a reviewer of this book, want to utilize the opportunity to connect with readers for strengthening their quantumatic preceptions. To start a fantasy series of charismatic social changes, the writer of this book expressed her creative views reamarkably in the following sixteen proses: - Pandan; Platform of Neem-tree; Comeback; Wild Herb; Life's Dusk; Tai Ji; Ship Bird; Sappo; Half Land Half Sky; Coward; Enough! Now No More; Crackling Relationships; That Stranger; New Dawn; Party Night; and Caretaker.

Pandan, Comeback and Tai ji these three stories sketched on the pattern of human-science in which humanities has become much more fruitful. Mutual social influences have came across the lightening of these stories where humanity and imapartequal diskette of humanity have constantly influenced with each other.

Stories like Half Land Half Sky and Crackling Relationships are totally influenced by the new societial scientific ideas. These two have been coined with some highly odysseus space and designed on the pattern of imaginatic un-robotic behaviour.

Literary science outreach on one of the best story 'Enough! Now No More'. This story has been designed on the cultural sphere with society architectural base. The renaissance of relationship between person and family more significantly shown in this story which affects everybody mind effecting trapical science changes. My Voltairic exordium stick to this which agrees with the mindful creations. Varous type of chemical bondings have been illustrated in this story. Hence, book's name based on this story is true the best sense of this literary work.

I extend my thanks to the writer for providing me the opportunity to write this 'Exordium' and I am happy to share my view as cited above of this book with all you readers.

~ Editor
(Ganvru Pramod)
Noida (India), Delhi-NCR
Dated : 23.06.2024

Acknowledgements

I am very thankful to well known Hindi Litterateur 'Granvru Pramod' for his immense support in the process of this book writing.

Madhushri K.

CHAPTER ONE

NEW DAWN

"Hey girl, where are you going without asking?"

"I want to meet your Babuji," said Kusuma, shaking the peon's hand.

"Who Babuji?"

"Hey! That's our Tehsildar Babu."

"He is not here, he has gone out for some work and he don't met any stranger, tell me what is the work?

"I won't tell you."

"Come on, then run away from here."

The peon said very rudely and pushed her out of the gate. It had been four days since Kusuma had been circling the Tehsildar's porch. Till now she had not been able to succeed in the task of conveying the complaint to Tehsildar Saheb which her mother had assigned her.

Kusuma was a fatherless daughter whose mother's eyesight was slowly dying. She was taking care of her mother like a mother. She was a fifteen year old teenager. Fate had prematurely brought her to the threshold of the responsible age of twenty-five years.

She walked towards home muttering, 'today I am too tired to go to the kiln.'

She was scolding herself in her mind. Every day, to keep her mother's mind, she used to rub her nose on the Tehsildar's doorstep, which she did not like at all. It was very difficult for the innocent person who was playing a game of hide and seek with her to recognize the wolves sitting in the group of men.

Mother's eye medicine had become run out and she didn't even have money. After thinking something, she turned towards the kiln. Chhedi Lal was sitting in front, smoking a pipe. Chedi was a favourite and honest man of the kiln owner. When he came here in search of work, he must have been seventeen years old. He became a mason from a bojhwa labourer, then the owner was happy and promoted him and he started handling all the work along with the accountants' work and the surveyor of the kiln. He became a family member. He and his wife live in a room built in the courtyard of the kiln. The only son is Bittan Singh, whom his parents fondly call Bittu, who after completing his studies in the city, works as a supervisor in a company.

Recently he had come home. There was a dispute over some issue between the owner and the workers in the company where he worked. The factory work was almost closed, so he had taken a few days' leave and came home.

Seeing Kusuma coming in front... "Why did you come in the evening, laddo?" Chedi asked in a loving tone.

"That prickly uncle is like this, mother's medicine has run out. If you would give some money in advance..." Kusuma said flatteringly.

"How much you need" Without waiting for a reply he handed a two hundred rupee note into her hand.

"Come tomorrow on time."

"Yes uncle, I will come for work tomorrow", saying this she started going out.

Seeing Bittan Singh sitting on a chair outside the gate of the kiln, she stopped for a moment as if she was feeling 'recognised'. She was trying to put some pressure on her mind to remember that... He (Bittan) disrupted her thoughts.

"Nakko! won't you talk to me?"

She was shocked saying

"shit!"

Hearing 'Nakko', she also remembered that three-legged langur whose hanging long tail she used to pull behind and tease him by saying 'Langur came, langur came' and he used to go tearful to his

Baba to complain. There was a strange tickle buried in some corner of her mind, turned into the redness of ten roses, and landed on her chubby cheeks, but ignoring this, she quickly walked towards home to get the medicine for her mother's eyes.

"Baba, she is the same naughty girl, isn't she? When she was little, she used to dominate everyone and used to do less work and used to sleep more on the furnace. Her nostrils would keep moving all the time. If I teased her by calling her Nakko, she would run to bite me like a cat." Bittan said making Kusuma laugh.

"Yes, this is the same fate-stricken girl. Her father had passed away many years ago. She is carrying the entire burden on her shoulders and supporting herself and her mother. But there should never be a wrinkle on the girl's face nor should anyone complain. Just keep smiling always. Fate is also the guide of time, son, close your eyes and walk with time right and left, she does not see whether the shoulder on which she will place the yoke of havoc is that of a young girl or a young man.

*

Kusuma's father Hukum Singh and her younger brother Muluk Singh both lived with their family very lovingly. There was a lot of love between the two brothers. There was no difference between farming and food together, but between their wife's relations, the relationship of sisters-in-laws was only for showing.
*

"Look brother, get up, today you have to go to the city to buy seeds, have you forgotten?"

Hukum shook his younger brother who was sleeping very deeply. Muluk sat up as soon as he heard his elder brother's voice.

"Yes brother, today I slept so much that I lost consciousness in the morning, I wanted to tell you one thing, our servant Ram Lal said that there is some fault in the motor of the tube well, these days it has to make more noise. "

"Yes, you will have to go and see. Now you get up early, have bread and water and go to the city." Saying this, Hukum went to work.

Hukum's outfit was as simple as Angooridei's, minding her own business, while Chhota's outfit, Ramiya, was as simple as hers. Ramiya, who has passed 10th class, thumbs her illiterate thumb in front of her sister-in-law and does not let anyone lay a hand on her, as if after passing 10th class, she has become everyone's master by having the complete knowledge of studies in her hands. She had become a one-eyed queen among the blind. She used to look down on the illiterate Angoori and did not leave any chance to humiliate her, but there was a pain which kept on rattling in her heart, that was the girl playing in her sister-in-law's lap. Seeing her, she felt sorry for her empty lap. Ramiya, who did not consider herself inferior to anyone, would get defeated here and her pride which always raised its hood and was ready to sting everyone, at that time, forgetting to hiss at others, she would enter into her own nest and she leaves no stone unturned to attack others.

Muluk was also fed up with the daily fights; he had not left any doctor or midwife in the town. Where was he going to see the anger of a woman of a man's caste? There would be fights every day, but even Ramiya, who failed for the fourth time, was not going to get into the anger of her man. One day, in anger, when Muluk raised his hand on her, the lioness sharpened her claws more and one day, fed up with the daily squabbles, she went to her mother's home and never returned. Muluk went to get her twice but his in-laws' door was slammed on his face and he was chased away like a dog. Injured by the insult of Wife, Muluk became ferocious like a dog that has not got even a loaf of bread by showing a piece of bone. Muluk, like a loose bull without a yoke, lost his way. Fighting with brothers and sisters-in-law at home is more important than farming work. With the stolen desires, he got addicted to the comfort of bread and illicit food and started living in the company of an unruly Patwari where there were feasts of chicken and liquor every day.

Greed and ill-intentioned bribery have created such a dent in relationships that it has started eating away at not only the boundary walls but also the foundation.

It so happened that the Patwari of the village filled the mind of the younger brother Muluk with such a poison of greed against the order that in the beginning there was a squabble between the two brothers, whereas Muluk used to consider his elder brother as his father, but now he is very harsh. But it came down. Slowly the four stoves got separated, the water pipes also got divided and a high wall stood in the middle of the hall.

The evacuation routes of both became North-South. But the agricultural land had not been divided yet. Years passed by so, hence Hukum started working alone as much as he could. But sometimes luck struck that the crop did not grow completely, sometimes hailstorms or droughts hit. Ram Lal, a loyal man who had been doing farming for years. He too went back to his village. When a ship sinks, not only people but even rats start running away. He also shed the filth of his loyalty and ran away to his village.

One night, Angoori and her daughter were hit by such a dark storm that it took away the roof over their heads and ruined their lives overnight. Angoori's husband slept so hard at night that he did not wake up in the morning. It didn't understand by anyone what happened in the night.

*

In a house where for years there was a train full of Egyptian batons every day, today both mother and daughter had to break their chains to earn bread.
Ten year old Kusuma had understood that she should do some work because uncle Muluk had also withdrawn his hand. For some time, he kept sending a little grain by his own man, but gradually it also reduced and it became difficult for the mother and daughter to feed themselves. One day Angoori sent Kusuma to Muluk.

"Why? My parts became so useless that as soon as he (my husband) left, my perspective changed. I should also have my share in the land, it should be my full right. There is no respect in your eyes, so what happened? By whom did you fall into the trap, my dear brother? "Doesn't your heart melt even after seeing Lalli?"
"I am not under anyone's influence. If nature betrays me again and

again, what can I do? The gold-spewing land has been devoured by the evil eye.

I can definitely give you a piece of advice that you should employ Lalli somewhere or arrange for her marriage, else you will leave her in trouble and, listen! she studied a lot, now she should stop going to school. I told the teacher that our daughter will no longer come to her school. I have studied five grades, that's enough, if I fail in fourth, I will do all the work." Saying this, he started laughing.

"Look Muluk, I don't know anything about all this, give me your share of pride or money."

"Listen to what I say, I am not the girl's enemy."

Muluk had his eyes fixed on Angoori's face and wanted to take advantage of the opportunity.

"Look, the Patwari of the village is like this, he is my friend, he is not very old, he is still eligible for marriage, if you ask then Lalli will marry him...."

Muluk could not even finish talking when Angoori screamed loudly. "Beware of anyone who utters even a single word. How can you talk? What is the age of this girl! How she might get married at this age."

"Think about it." Saying this, Muluk got up and left.

Muluk's talk was creating confusion in Angoori's mind. Angoori would get worried after seeing twenty-one beauties of the community in appearances and complexions.

'Nasty people are keeping an eye on the fatherless daughter, but I will never let this happen. I will work as a labourer but will not push my daughter into the well.'

Both mother and daughter were somehow pulling the cart of their lost time. Mother started working as a house worker or housemaid in the houses and Kusuma used to collect fruits, flowers and berries from the garden and bushes and used to sit outside the door of the house to sell them but she soon realized that this would not be enough. One day she came to know that in the village a brick factory was going to be set up. She reached there without informing her mother. When she appealed to the owner, he did not listen but his man Chhedi Lal took pity on her and hired her. It would have been a great satisfaction to the poor man's heart to get her to do some light work and pay her some wages secretly from the employer.

Slowly time passed and with time Kusuma became young. Now if she worked honestly, the burden on Chedi's mind would also become lighter.

*

"O mother! Take medicine, hold it. The medicine-man was saying that the medicine has to be put in the eye daily, otherwise the sore eye will not get cured soon."

After handing over the medicine bottle to her mother, she went into the kitchen and saw two roasted potatoes.

'Maybe mother might have buried it in the barn'

Kusuma prepared bhurta by adding salt and pepper and consumed the remaining rotis from the night.

She took it and sat down to eat with her mother.

"Amma, don't cry. Look at the condition of your eyes. Open your ears and listen. I am only your daughter. As for my marriage, I have told you not to marry anyone. I should not go anywhere leaving you."

She consoled her mother, but every night while lying on the bed, she felt the breaking of the swing of dreams in which she used to swing higher and higher during her childhood and youth. She knew that one day her thread would definitely get strained. She would be devastated because neither could she dare to turn away from her responsibility nor did she have the courage to do so.

*

This morning Kusuma had opened her eyes early but she did not feel like leaving her cot. She was silently staring at the ceiling beams, adding and subtracting yesterday and today.

"What's the matter, Lado? Will you not go to work today? Is it okay?"

"No Amma, it's nothing special, I just have pain in my legs."

"No problem, don't go today" Angoori with great love started caressing her daughter's head.

*

"Listen, girl's one anklet's anklet has broken. Bring a new one and yes, this time bring an anklet with nice thick anklets. This will bring glory to our house, when she walk chirping in the courtyard, and for seeing this we will get a chill in our chest."
Hukum picked up Kusuma in his lap, who was playing nearby.
"Hey, what can you talk about, I will also bring a silver case with small curls, I will load my daughter with jewelery and I will marry her in such a house where my daughter will rule."

*

'A delicate little girl and a dense distress too much', leaving me in the middle, he himself went far away with his legs spread.
"What are you thinking? Get up, give me something to eat and then I'll go to work, it's already very late."

*

After completing the work at the kiln, she stood outside the gate of the Tehsildar's office and was thinking that if the bastard uncle had not betrayed her, she would not have had to suffer so many blows. Even today the Patwari's laundress sent her back from outside.

"Neither Patwari Saheb nor Bade Saheb is there and listen to one thing, girl! Higher officer has gone out. We will meet you after a month. Now you stop roaming around here."
Saying this he closed the gate.

*

"Look brother, I have done a good job for you, but you have not kept your promise," Patwari said, hitting Muluk's shoulder hard.

"What should I do, I tried a lot, so to speak, she seems to be my sister-in-law, but she should not let anyone lay hands on her and certainly not in relation to her daughter."

"I don't know anything, see, the ball is still in your court. Somehow please convince the girl, otherwise you also know what I can do." Muluk was shocked to see the harsh tone of the Patwari. At that time, he thought it best to leave from there with his tail tucked like a dog, but his dishonest and crooked brain started searching for some new trick.

*

There was a deal between Patwari and Muluk that if Kusuma would marry him then he would transfer the fields belonging to his elder brother to him. But circumstances, wives and lands are such that these do not take long for good intentions to get spoiled. The gaze that was fixed on the girl also got stuck on her land.

Patwari did the work of Muluk but for his own benefit. By measuring the land wrongly with a dishonest pen, the dishonest man transferred half of the land of the two brothers to his own name and the remaining half to Muluk. The foolish and greedy Muluk could not understand his trick.

The mother and daughter had no idea what conspiracy was being carried out against them.

She (Kusuma) was upset with the fact that her uncle had become dishonest and was greedy in his mind, that is why he was not giving them their share of food grains. Kusuma was making rounds of the government office every day with a petition complaining about this.

'Once the higher officer is reprimanded, uncle will improve. Grains ripping time has came but not a single piece of grains reached to her house.' Ten types of questions were arising in her mind. Thinking this, Kusama walked towards the fields. 'If I see, the land is in ruins or some animals are grazing in the farm.'

The month of Phagun, amidst the rosy cold, the lukewarm gust of the gusting wind was awakening hopes of happiness in her mind. Taking long steps, she reached her farm. Muluk was sitting on a chair in front, smoking hookah with the Patwari.

"What did you do here, girl? Did you drink all the solution out of shame? What is the use of women in farming?"

"I came here just to see, uncle, how this year's crop has been. You see very thick pearl earrings here and you say that grains have not born, the land has become infertile."
"Nowadays you have started talking too much. Keep quiet and go home otherwise..."
Now Kusuma had started to understand that her uncle's intentions had gone wrong. Now she would have to complain about this brain-dead uncle to the bigger government.

*

"Have you come again?" the peon said reprimandingly and then paused for a while and spoke.
"Okay, tomorrow morning you come, I will introduce you to Sahab."
Next day she reached office early in the morning.
"Come, Sahab is inside." Kusuma followed him.
   She went inside and saw the same man sitting on the chair who was smoking hookah with his uncle on the farm yesterday.
"I don't want to meet him, I want to meet Sahab."
"This is Sahab." Saying this he went out.
   Surrounded by the fog of doubt, she started looking for a way out. When the wolf felt that the prey was slipping away, he moved forward and tried to hold her hand. A tingling current ran through Kusuma's entire body. She freed her hand and went to the corner and stood there. Shivering like a Lajwanti plant, Kusuma started praying in her mind to all the before and after Gods and Goddesses. She had not expected this moment at all. She felt weak for a moment and then regained her composure, kindling the heat of the furnace of hard work. She collected all her strength. She stood up holding her breath, saying 'I am not a lump of clay, after picking up bricks and stones, even virility has now become not made of bones but made of stone, if anyone does anything wrong, I will not waste a moment in pressing to the dead body.'
"Pitch ..."
Spitting the betel leaf in a corner, he tried to control his saliva and look good because he knew that the whole game could be spoiled in

a hurry.

"Hey, sit down! Don't be afraid! Tell me what's you want."

"Get me file a report against my uncle. He himself should eat all the grains from my father's land, there is nothing wrong, except cheating and trickery by him."

"Tell me your father's name."

"Hukum Singh S/o Ram Singh."

He said while flipping through his papers, "this man doesn't even have any farm in his name. O girl! You have misunderstood something, or you have forgotten your father's name." Saying this, he threw the first die on the chessboard.

"Sir! No one can even forget his father's name. Hasn't your mind been killed? You should not feel ashamed by making such a crude joke on the woman caste."

Growling like a lioness, Kusuma quickly ran away from there without wasting a moment. She had understood the game of collusion between the powerfuls. Fuming with anger, Kusuma went straight to the kiln.

While narrating the dark deeds of the enemies to Chhedi Lal, she hugged him and cried bitterly. Bittan was standing in a corner silently listening to everything. It seemed as if someone had noticed the rose-like laughter that blooms in every season. The girl whom everyone had always seen laughing was disintegrating like a withered flower surrounded by thorns. Today he was clearly realizing the mystery of why his heart was becoming so distressed after seeing her sorrow. Chedi Lal was shocked as soon as he heard it, his tongue was stuck to the roof of his mouth.

"Such darkness will not do. You might have henna on your hands, but we don't have it on our hands, nor are we wearing bangles. Don't panic, keep quiet," Bittan said while consoling Kusuma. He felt like going ahead and holding her hand and saying, 'Don't worry, I am here.' The thing that had been suppressed in his mind for years, which he had neither understood nor been able to say, came out of his mouth today.

"Don't worry! I'll see." Then he paused for a while and said...

"Let me drop you home."
'I am coming, Baba!', he said to Chedi and went out. When he looked back, he saw Kusuma following him with a downcast gaze.

*

"It won't work, it won't work, Gunda Raj won't work."
Early in the morning, after hearing the noise of slogans outside her house, Kusuma came out and saw that Bittan along with his fellow labourers had gathered outside her house with a stick in one hand and a black band tied on the other arm and were raising slogans. For a moment she could not believe that the first ray of the morning had brought a new message for her, now that she was not alone.
The procession of her colleagues marched across the town shouting slogans and stopped outside the Tehsildar's office.

Today, luck was with Kusuma, in order to trap her, the powerful Patwari and her uncle had been making dozens of lies by bribing the peon. Today, seeing the huge crowd of protesters outside the office and the sticks in their hands, he felt sad. He lost his senses. He thought it best to follow the path of truth and took the pamphlet from Kusuma's hand and placed it on the Tehsildar's table.

When the Tehsildar Saheb, who was unaware of the matter of dishonest land grabbing, got the inquiry done, the whole lie came to light that the Patwari had bad intentions, he had an eye on both, the girl and the farm, and wanted to take control of them by any means. The office peon revealed the whole truth and the Patwari was dismissed and sent to jail. Uncle Muluk's condition was such that after the flood water recedes, rotten and smelling debris remains; no one even likes to stand near him. He was not able to show his face to anyone in the town, no one knew when and where he had gone.

*

"From today onwards you are discharged from the kiln job." Bittan stood proudly blocking Kusuma's path.
"Why uncle? What is he saying? Don't do such atrocities, tell me my

mistake." Kusuma became tearful.

Bitton was enjoying watching the changing expressions on Kusuma's face.

"Won't you make roti and feed me and Baba?"

As soon as she raised her eyes and looked towards Bittan...

She could not stand before the magical siren

"Hey!" she said and ran towards the house feeling shy.

*****

CHAPTER TWO

HALF LAND HALF SKY

There is neither any kind of criteria nor the criteria of being a woman or a man to be fertilized by feelings. But when there is a flood of feelings, then it does not see the man or the woman. Even the feeling of someone's incomplete existence gets blossomed and spreads its fragrance till the horizon. This is the story of such an incomplete woman.

Aniket alias Chanda was preparing to go to college. By the way, he used to wake up every day at six in the morning, it was his mother's order to wake up every morning and chant the Lord's name, do some exercise and thereafter start daily routine. Today eyes don't open, it open with mother's phone, when he wakes up, he sees it is his mother's phone. "Hello mother, how are you? Is everything fine this morning, isn't it?" "Yes, everything is fine, how are you Chanda? How are your studies going?""I am fine mother, now it is the final year, just then your Chanda will be with you"."Yes son, if the Lord has mercy".

The phone got disconnected in the middle. Aniket got busy in his daily work and had to reach the college on time, but the mind became somewhat reluctant since the mother's talk was left incomplete. He Went to college but didn't like there too. He had three periods but came to the room after attending onle two periods. Somewhere something was missing which was making him restless. He called mother, the bell kept ringing, but no answer came. He started getting nervous, now he could not feel well.

Mother had sent him to study far away, there was an order to come home once a year, but today the mind was not ready to obey any order. Although Sujanpur was not very far away from Hamirpur, it must have been twenty-five to thirty kilometers. He had to come and go by bus and for this there was a lot of fighting during the course of travelling .

After completing his studies at Sainik School in Sujanpur, Aniket was given wings to fly by his mother by sending him to Hamirpur Engineering College. He didn't know when he fell asleep sitting in the bus swinging in the carousel of childhood memories."Hey brother, get up, Sujanpur Teehra has arrived, let's get down quickly"- the conductor's voice suddenly opened his eyes. He got off from the bus and walked on foot. Today even the way to home seemed long. The condition of the roads had become worse than before. Aniket was getting annoyed with the local administration. Somehow reached home and was shocked to see the door locked. A man came out from the neighborhood silently handed over the key and closed the door.

Aniket thaught, mother was not knowing that he I was coming. No problem, today mother has to be surprised. She will take scolding, no matter what he will be scolded. Opening the lock, he saw that the whole room was full of sunshine, as if the sun rays coming from the window were welcoming him. Mother's picture was kept in front, it was very old, once she had stubbornly shotted it out. Lying on the mother's bed he started waiting for her, only then he saw that some pages were twisted and broken near the picture, but kept very neatly."My Chanda! I knew that you would come because I know you more than you, I am not your mother, I am your fault for what I am going to tell you, because I kept a dark corner of my heart hidden from you. And kept its door always closed for you, I am responsible, forgive me my son. Today I take you to my past fifty years ago. I was born in Delhi's middle class educated family. Father used to work in a small company. We were three brothers and sisters. I had a sister older than me and a brother younger than me. All three of us siblings were very happy under the shadow of our parents. Among all the three siblings, I was very intelligent in studies. Everyone loved me very much, but the course of time changed in such a way that suddenly a storm came in my life. I was that flower which was removed from his garden by the gardener himself. Then I was a child, I could not know what was my fault. I cried a lot, I remember at that time my mother fainted crying. My brother was roaring and the elder sister, she was standing like a scared statue. It was only my gardener i.e. my father who had become stone hearted. I was handed over to a stranger. Just like, someone trying to save his plant by uprooting the weeds and throws them away. I thought my father had sold me, but this is the truth, which I was also unaware of. I came to know much later that what was my fault, which I did not do and for which I have been punished. I was handed over to those people who used to do the work of dancing and singing. I had accepted this fate's joke. There was another girl of my age there. After meeting her it seemed that what had happened to me had also happened to her. God has sent both of us to the earth but without completing it, perhaps he has forgotten, like a toy maker makes a mistake while making a toy, makes one or the other part ugly or forgets to attach a part. Although I was beautiful to look at but what to say to you, my son! Well that other girl's name was Kukku. My school's and home's name was Gayatri. The people I had to live with had changed my name too like my life. I was changed from Gayatri to Gato. Kukku and me were the wingless birds tied with a single branch, who could not fly even if wanted to fly. Year after year, playing music and spreading hands while standing at the red light was the only life, but the memory of home was the same that I used to get snake bites every night. It used to keep biting like this. Day and night the life was going on like this.

One day at night, I was returning to my camp with my friends, when I heard the cry of a child, I looked here and there, I could not see anything, all my friends went ahead, but my mind got stuck. I went back there again and saw a little boy wrapped in a cloth crying loudly behind the garbage container. For a long time I was confused about what to do and what not to do. I felt that day that in some corner inside my heart a thief named Mamta was sitting hiding. My son! I brought you home hiding in my lap. Brought you home and showed you to all the friends in my fear. Everyone was happy, everything went on well for a few days. Our chief also did not say anything. I was very happy. It was as if I had got a drop of nectar, only a drop of which could revive me. There was enough to keep. Only a few days had passed.

One day Kukku said- Kukku :- "Gato/Gayatri! you go away from here."Gato/Gayatri:- "Why? what happened, where do I go? My house has also been snatched away"Kukku:- "No, no, you either hand over this child to them or go somewhere with your child. I have heard that these people were talking that they want to mutilate this child and make them like themselves. They want to include him in their community. That's why I am telling you to go somewhere with the child."

My son! It was as if the sky had fallen on me. Time has changed in such a way that everything changed in a moment. The house which I had adopted considering my luck, today the same house seemed to be imprisoned. Once again I was leaving the house but I was satisfied that this time I did something. For which I was being punished and I was happily ready to face this punishment.

My son! One night in the dark, I set out on a new journey with you. I did not know where the vehicle I was sitting would take me! The journey had taken me far away from my land and I used to get bumped in train and sometimes in bus, now the name of the land on which I am standing, is Sujanpur Teehra.

My son! I kept wandering here and there hiding my identity in the midst of strange people and strange places. Time was testing me at every step and I was searching for my destination. I kept stumbling but I didn't want to live by begging. I kept wandering in search of work, and got work in a hotel doing utensils' cleaning.

My Chanda! due to your luck, one day a Seth and Sethani came to that hotel. I don't know whether he felt pity on me or his heart ached seeing you little one in my lap, otherwise everyone hates my caste and my community. I got the job of cooking food in that Seth's house. I would not call it a drowning straw. Yes, I had found a boat full of possibilities which made my journey easy. I was very happy with this new change in life. I must have had some previous birth relation with Sethani whom I used to call Baijee.

My son! This turn of life taught me to be proud of myself. Till now the frustration of the neglected and despised life which had become like a banyan tree in the mind, has been dried up and fallen in a few days. You made me sit on the mother's throne.

My son! you came into my life as an angel. Slowly years passed by, I could not read, fate and time did not allow me to read."

Aniket does not know how long he sobbed while reading, his heart wanted to come out by ripping open his chest neglected by the fraternity. Then he started crying loudly.

"No, no, she is my mother" saying this Aniket pulled himself. He could not stop, he started reading every page of this book of life, which was writing a new story for him. He too was a victim of neglect by someone who had left him to die. Saying mother mother, he started crying bitterly.

"My son! I know it must be very difficult for you to accept all this, but the truths of life that fate brings us face to face, be it sweet or bitter, we have to accept both. This is the life. When I sent you outside to study further, I sent you with a stone on my chest, whereas the stone kept sinking inside me and slowly destroying me."

Aniket noticed that once he came home during the holidays, he found his mother very weak, but she used to go to work equally, so he did not pay much attention at that time. At that time Aniket said, "Mother! you don't eat food behind me, do you?"Gayatri :- "Why don't you eat, if I don't eat food then how will I work."Aniket :- "I feel like this, may be you haven't slept properly even at night. If you have any problem, why don't you tell me? Tomorrow you go to see the doctor, then I will leave. You will not do anything."Gayatri :- "Oh! no, I am fine, if something happens, Baijee is there. I will tell her, she will show me to a doctor, don't worry at all."Saying this, the mother postponed and the matter ended there. He thought that he also forgot to go there and got busy in his studies. Today he was feeling that "Let the mother come, this time he will definitely take her to the doctor." Strange thoughts started coming in his mind. Again he shook his eyes on the letter.

"My son! Now I have only one wish that you become a big man after studying. Of course, you would not mention me to anyone, but my presence will always remain in some corner of your heart. You have made me worthy, but My son! you have come into my life. I will not be able to reciprocate the happiness and joy that you have given me for many births. May you always be happy. My son! I can't say that my age will be with you."

Now the dam of Aniket's patience was breaking. He thaught, what is happening! I will have to go and ask Baijee. And as soon as he stood up to go (to Baijee), two people entered inside the house. He asked who are you? Mother is not at home. On hearing this, a person who looked like a woman started crying bitterly. "Hi! Hi! Gato! where have you gone?"

Destiny was understanding who was mourning for whom, but Aniket was not able to understand this, hence he started saying- "Where is my mother?" Kukku:--" My name is Kukku, I am your mother's friend. Your mother has left all of us and now she will never come again." Aniket :- "What are you saying, I had talked to her yesterday only. Tell me quickly what happened thereafter? Where is she, take me to her."Kukku :-- "Your mother had lung disease. She didn't tell anyone, not even me. She was ill for many years. It was just a whim that she doen't tell about. It was just for you so that you will not leave your studies and come back. She also told me a few days back. She had suddenly informed me two days back and immediately called me. When I came here, I saw that she was a guest for a few moments in this land. That time she told me that after her death, her rituals should be done before the arrival of her son. She does not want that in the next birth too she should become an incomplete woman. She wants the whole sky to live. Again She started saying that if her son saw her dead body, then he will have to become a eunuch in the next life as well. Saying this she left the world. As is the custom, we buried her at night. It was a compulsion in our society, it is a practice that if someone sees our soil, we will get the same body again. Now tell me, have I made any mistake in this? Son! now you pray for the peace of her soul, may be her wish be fulfilled and you may be born from her womb in the next life."

Saying this, Kukku started crying bitterly. Aniket hugged Kukku chest as if his mother's heart would be found beating in this chest."Have patience, son! pray that the wish of that unfortunate person is fulfilled". Having said this, Kukku hid Aniket in her chest.

*****

CHAPTER THREE

COWARD

It would not have been even ten minutes since Reema came to the park that a boy who must have been eight or nine years old, extending his hand towards her, he said, "Madam, this is for you.""For me! Who gave?" Reema asked holding the paper."It is not known, I don't know, he has gone and he asked to give it to you."

***

The pages of the past started opening spontaneously in Reema's mind..."Reema you are sitting here" Isha said hitting Reema's shoulder."I didn't find you anywhere, even went to the library, I thought I would get my nerd there.""Hey why, what is the matter that I was so searched for? Two consecutive periods were free, so I came and sat here. See how good it is, you come and sit too.""You didn't find it that day in Shakespeare's Macbeth Library, someone had taken it. Actually Vikram Rai had taken this book and that day he must have seen that you were looking for this book, so today instead of returning it, he was saying that I will give it to you. Read it and return it to him." "Vikram! Who is he?""Hey, that senior Vikram who is also my cousin brother from a distant relation.""Well done.""Listen, I am on my way, it is my class-period, otherwise Joshi ma'am's brows will go up" saying this Isha went away.

Reema was in no hurry to go home today. Mother and father have gone to see the younger uncle. A day earlier, the aunt had called that he was not feeling well. They both got off in the next bus. Reema was thinking for how long can she sit here too. Even as the sun started going downhill, in the month of October, as soon as the day ends, Reema thought it is better to get up. She caught the bus and came home.

Reema had a habit of reading something or the other before going to bed at night, which was not from today but for the past many years. She had found the book she had been looking for for a long time and very curiously she turned on the side lamp of her bed to read the book. As soon as she opened the book, a pink piece of paper was kept folded on the first page, thinking that the person who must have read this book had some important paper left. She picked that paper and kept it on a side table, but every time her mind used to go to that paper 'What do I want to do, for me it is just a paper'. The night had already passed and her eyes were getting heavy from sleep, so she kept the same paper in the book like a book-mark that it would be easy to read from here tomorrow, but the curiosity of her mind again raised its head and stood up 'Let me see what is this right, it may be someone's laundry bill or receipt of some goods, whose this tomorrow she will give it to him.'"I want to meet you Rima" Vikram.

Complete paper was blank, only one line! For a few moments Reema became numb and suddenly someone threw a pebble in the calm water and created a stir. Reema vaguely remembered that once she too had attended Isha's birthday party, when Isha had introduced her to one Vikram Rai, that too in a cursory manner, and never met again after that. "There was never anything worth remembering in him, and there is not even today. Is this not the same Vikram? I do not know any other Vikram." Reema switched off the lamp and started trying to sleep, but today's untoward incident did not let her sleep, the whole night she was in turmoil and her one mind says, "Hey, he wants to meet, what is the big deal"Then the other mind would raise it head and says, 'If he wanted to meet, he would have come and met her in front of everyone, why was there any need to send such a message secretly?" "Ok I'll see, I will talk to Isha tomorrow, now go to sleep, you silly girl"....thinking this, when did her eyes widen, it is not known.

When she opened her eyes in the morning, she was in a hurry to reach the college, as if a decision was about to be made in the court, and the life of the plaintiff was stuck, it is not known what decision would come out. Isha was not seen in the class that day, but the sight of one man was coming again and again and then she saw Isha who was talking to that man. Standing by the railing, Reema was very confused that just then... "Reema! Today you became late and missed one period" saying this and holding the hand of Reema and taking her in front of Vikram, Isha said,"Reema, he is brother Vicky. You have probably met him before. I am noticing this, why?"Reema was unconcerned about everything as if she didn't hear anything. There was a conflict of questions and answers going on inside her, heart wanted to ask Isha why her brother wanted to meet her, but as if by locking her tongue, untouchable emotions were trying to defeat her by playing with her heart. Reema wanted to look at Vicky with a frown, but he was looking at her. Reema got confused, just then Isha also gone to attend class period by talking to other girl. Reema also wanted to walk from there, but what was the hypnosis of the stranger's face standing in front of her eyes that was pulling her towards him and not letting her move from there. It seemed as if his eyes wanted to get the answer to the question from Reema's eyes which he had not yet asked.Reema wanted to break the silence, she was afraid that the suffocating tide of swearing silence inside might burst suddenly and become the cause of an accident."Why do you want to meet me, Vikram ji?"The way Vikram looked at her, Reema shuddered because there was an unknown invitation in his eyes that stirred Reema's heart for which she was not ready at all."What should I say, you ask yourself and what you are also unaware of, the same thing is clearly visible in your eyes." No answer was understood by Reema, as if blood without any cut and her situation became in strange. What and how did this happen in one night and with what authority is the silent language of someone's eyes daring to enter in her inner self. Has the destiny forced the stubborn outburst of her emotions to accept her defeat and surrender?

Reema left for home early from college and got down before today at the bus stop where she used to get down. The way to home was looking good today. The beautiful evening of pink cold was soaking the body and mind with the joy of unknown happiness and the heart was wishing that it should keep moving with the warmth of these romantic thoughts and that this time and path should never end, just then the horn of someone's car from behind woke her up from a raw sleep with a jolt. She realized her mistake that she was walking in the middle of the road. After saying sorry, she sat on the bench made on the footpath for some time. The hypnosis of Vikram's eyes had taken hold of her entire being. Within two days she had become a stranger to herself and she was liking this strangeness.

Reema and Vikram started meeting frequently. In some time Reema had come to know that this person is of a different nature. Extremely shy and lost, this person who remains silent leaves a mark of his presence in the surrounding environment. There is something in this person that separates him from others. Reema had also learned to read his silence very well. The vine of love's sympathy was searching for its loving support, clinging to which it could reach its destination."Now what are you thinking about next?""Yes, I will talk at home. Give me some time. It takes time for inter-caste relations to be recognized. Anyway, my family is a little bit more conservative, but don't you worry.""Look, you have to find a solution for this, you have to talk. You have to persuade them.""Yes, yes, after the final exam, I am going home and will talk. I will try my best to convince. You can rest assured."

***

After Vikram left, Reema got busy with her studies and there was still one more year left for the finals. After Vikram's departure, calls kept coming every week. Reema was also waiting to hear the happy news along with his phone call. Vicky's thoughts were not letting her fly anywhere and now an unknown fear started surrounding her. Her finals were also completed but the relationship between the two could not reach any destination. She got a call after a long time..."What's the matter Vicky? Tell me, is it okay?""Yes, I am trying to give you the good news, I have got a job.""?""Hey why are you silent? Aren't you happy?""It has become very good, now it is like you come and meet my father. I talked to him, he wants to meet you.""Okay, I'll come."Now Reema is relieved but this too could not last for long.Gradually, Vicky's phone calls reduced, when Reema wanted to do so, the wrong number slapped all her hopes. Days, weeks, months went by, but the one who was supposed to come did not turn up. It was as if love had stopped, neither there was a coincidence nor a separation. The existence of femininity was only to be the fiefdom of father today, husband tomorrow and son in the last phase of life. Is this the ultimate truth of femininity? Stuck in these confusions, there was only one option in front of Reema, that wherever the wind takes her, keep flowing in the same flow. There is no such stage in the journey of life where it can be said 'O life, wait a moment, let me rest for a while'. To free her parents from their responsibility, Reema started on a new path considering unwanted, unknowing relationship as her destiny.

**

Reema started looking at the children playing in the park, reminiscing the memories of the past, then noticed the leaflet in her hand.... When Reema opened it, she laughed and was also surprised. It was written "Khul Ja Sim Sim" Someone joked that the age above sixty is not the age to flirt.

Reema's daily rule was to come to the park and sit on the corner bench for some time and anyway the doctor has also said that to sit for some time in the sun, the knee pain has increased a little bit these days.

There is a lot of unrest in the house too, she was fed up with the daily fighting between the son and the daughter-in-law. As far as her role in the family is concerned, it is insignificant, she had no right to speak in any argument or quarrel in the house, she had no right to speak and just a roof was there over her head, and Reema was satisfied with that. The next day again the same boy came and handed over the paper and ran away. Today, the laugh didn't came instead she got annoyed, and what is the matter in the paper, she opened it..."Silence in solitude gives strength."Nice to read that who is this who is sending such a nice message. As it was his rule to come to the park, similarly it had become a rule for that child to run away every day holding a piece of paper which forced her to think who is this who is sending me such nice messages. He says that"Silence gives energy in solitude" and sometimes says "no one is alone in life, one's self is with one." Sometimes the message comes.."The disappointment of the present makes the future also dark, so avoid disappointment".

Reema also started feeling good after getting new positive messages daily, she started feeling change inside herself, she started feeling connected with some unknown relationship. The path of life, which seemed difficult and burdensome, now seems easy and she has started getting attached to her life. Waiting for the next day and the day the message does not come, the restlessness increases, she starts worrying that the stranger who is encouraging her indirectly, is he in some trouble?

Like this many days passed, one day she was returning home from the park, accidentally she saw the same boy, Reema could not help but immediately went and caught him."Listen son! haven't you come to the park for a long time?"There was a desire to ask and know a lot, but could not ask. The chain of dignity had bound the curiosities, she got drowned in thinking, that's time, the boy said..."Madam, that uncle has not come to the shop for many days, earlier he used to come to the shop every day to have tea, I don't know anything else, I work there, you go and ask the owner" said the boy pointing towards a shop. Reema's mind did not agree, her feet automatically moved towards that shop, when she went and asked, she came to know that the gentleman had not come there for many days, saying this, the tea-shop owner extended an envelope to her and said,"He has kept this envelope saying that if someone comes to ask me, then give it to her."Reema's heart started beating fast as if she was ready to go out. She sat there lifeless on the chair and opened the envelope with trembling hands."I'm sorry, I lost

the right to call you by your name years ago. I am still atonement for the crime of leaving you in the middle of the life's path. I can understand what must have happened to you after leaving you alone. I was scared at that time, I could not face the adverse circumstances, I did not have the courage to fight against the caste and society. I came to know later that you got married. I was satisfied in heart that now you are not alone. I still have a sense of guilt for not following my religion and by remaining unmarried for life, I am punishing myself for that crime even today and will continue to punish myself. My life is like a boat which moves in the same direction as the waves take it. One day suddenly saw you going to that park, you have changed a lot, you were looking very sad, your face was clearly telling your story. From people I came to know that your husband is also no more in this world. His first wife's son is taking care of you, how is he doing, it is written on your face. My crime is unforgivable, yet I am apologizing, it is said that the wish of the departed must be fulfilled. Don't know when------"
yours Vikram.

Reema took a deep breath and muttered softly, 'coward'

*****

CHAPTER FOUR

SAPPO

Sappo was quickly digging dung, that's why there was a sound..."Sappo! a little bit you look after the buffalo after digging dung. The buffalo has given birth today, hence you give water to Katia." "Yes Ma'am."After finishing the work, she had reached the gate that Kamdev was again blocking her way like everyday."Look what I got for you.""No, I don't want to see.""I have brought Jalebi for you, yoi try eating it.""Why? Do you my husband that you have been so kind to me?"

Kamdev started giggling and seeing his teeth stained with tobacco, Sappo was disgusted and she went silently outside towards looking him with angers in her eyes. When Kamdev did not seen anywhere for the next two days, Sappo understood that he had gone back to his village. It was good that the dead man was holding his nose that one day suddenly the ghost, i.e. Kamdev, again stood in front of her..."Look what a wonderful scented material I have brought for you."She ran away blushing like a young girl, she was in a hurry to reach home, ten days ago she had come to her saheb with golden dreams in her eyes.

****

Bhura, an old servant in the same haveli where Sappo works, is a very old servant of the Thakurani. Bhura is a very trusted man of the owner. Fought between the factory and the house to get bargains from the market, there is a lot of friction between the factory and the house, but his loyalty to his master never wavers.

And that's why he stayed here for years. There is a huge enclosure outside the haveli, in one corner of which cows and buffaloes are tied, and on the other hand, equal to the main gate, Bhura lives in the servant quarter. From here he also keeps watch of the house. Just a few days ago his nephew has come to the city in search of work. The search for work is just an excuse, he got so engrossed in the city's glare that he forgot the purpose of his coming. Hanging out with the street buffoon boys and living on his uncle's earning, it is his job. One day Sappo fell in front of him and while coming and going, his eyes fell on her.

The winter afternoon begins to set very quickly and Sappo wants to reach home before the day sets, that today again her way is blocked."Where did the wild cat go?"Kamdev does not leave any chance to tease Sappo and after hearing abuses from Sappo's mouth, the blood of that lash would have hit harder. Sappo also retorted and replied...."You, the hunter of wild rat, stay alive..."It seems that till Kamdev does not listen to her abuses, his bread cannot be digested."Your complain has to be made to ma'am, you bastard"Kamdev himself started laughing with hi..hi and went out whistling from the gate. After a while, he returns and sees Sappo sweeping the hallway."You are late, let me drop you home.""No I will go alone, no one will eat me.""If you find any wild cat.""It will not be dangerous like you."When Kamdev came close to her and started walking closely, Sappo cried out loudly."You go away.""Why? Is there any putridity in me? Your smell is just like dung since you are living with buffaloes. You look at me, how my clothes smell like jasmine!"

Sappo started thinking that this bastard tempts her everyday by showing scent, today he himself came after bathing in scent. Kamdev kept walking with her till half way, when he saw that her house was about to come, he started returning."Hey, where are you running? You won't meet your brother-in-law.""No, no, I'll see again"By giggling, he returned on the reverse foot.

   ***

This is the story of a girl who is the only shining star in the eyes of her three elder brothers and the pleasant coolness of her mother Sugna Dei and father Harkishan's chest, because Lakshmi ji was angry with many generations of this house. If anyone ever had a girl even before she was born, before opening her eyes, she would have left that house as a body of clay and would have been buried in the soil. Then what happened to Sappo's birth, the actual arrival of Lakshmi happened, even the kothi kuthala in the house started being filled with grains. The skilled craftsman of nature had sculpted the idol well, but shyam-colour had skimped on coloring her. The girl's body was dark or shyam-coloured since birth, but let it say that while climbing the ladder of teenage age, her body used to deceive people a lot with its brightness. The boisterous sea of dreams floating in the eyes of her sharp eyes, while roaring, would have been eager to drown everyone by pulling them towards it.

Coming to the threshold of youth, Sappo blossomed like a flower of evergreen and started enjoying herself in the world of her beauty. Mother father felt that the daughter had reached to the age of marriage. So they started looking for a groom for her."Look Sappo! Get ready well today, the boy's family is coming to see you."Naturally, the youth who was the authority of necklace decoration was going to stay behind, but in front of the dark complexion, even the sharp eyes and body-features did not work."Sappo! What happened in listening with the boy's family. Didn't you give any answer?"Sappo's mother Sugana Dei asked a question but seeing Harkishan's downcast face, she understood that the wedding procession has not yet come, but Sappo by being stone hearted, by being carefree of the worries of the world, is wandering with the prince of her dreams in her mayalok, she kept on doing as if only in this would be the end of her attainment of every happiness in her life. Sappo walks away from the world of reality by being Dears, she hums in the world of her dreams waiting for the prince of her dreams,"Mother! send me message Life is empty without lover."

Sappo, chirping in the courtyard like a Sonchiraiya and spreading auspiciousness in the house, giving coolness to the eyes of her brothers, but mother Sugana Dei was now worried day and night that the daughter who looked like a blossoming cowherd today might not dry up like a falling vine with time. Things were not going well in their caste and it would be an insult to their caste fraternity to have a girl in a lower caste than their own, but what was allowed to happen happened. Very far from own caste, i.e. from another caste, a relationship came for Sappo, which also brought the aura of a colorful rainbow hidden in the thick black clouds. Through Suganadei's distant aunt Ramdei, her neighbor Sadho Singh's young son Roshanlal's relationship has came. "O aunty! Namaste, why did you came?""Oye, you allow me to take a little bit breathe.""Yes, yes, take jaggery nuggets and drink water also."Ramdei came to the point after relaxing a little bit and after drinking cold water."Look, Sugna! Till when will you keep the girl sitting at home?""What should I do aunt, no relationship can be established between my daughter and other's sons. Let me say that the one with whom the knot will be tied will be found sooner or later by the grace of the Lord."

Aunt's brought relationship was not acceptable to anyone for their Lado i.e. Soppo. The boy used to work as a daily wage mechanic, sometimes he got job, and sometimes he didn't get it. This fear was coming in the way of every relationship came for Sappo."Is there any sure job?""What's of job, this will be sure with age, and your daughter is a fairy of Hoor, isn't she? So that, some saheb will come to marry her anyway. The girl's passionate age has reached to its extreme, how long will you keep her in the house?""Let's agree that going forward the job will be sure. But what about my community? Everyone will be angered, my food & water has also gone to their meeting.""Now it is not like that, who has time for this and anyway there is dirty stoves in every house," said the aunt while explaining.

Seeing good weather, Sappo was married as if the parents had taken a bath in the Ganges by taking off the burden of their chest and Sappo had found her husband, a handsome village young, whose golden wheat color makes his Roshan name meaningful, and for whom she used to dream of for years. After a month of marriage, she was getting gauna.

Pairs of colourful eleven honeymooners, pots and pans, sweets filled with father's, brother's pampering, pulses, ghee oil, sweets etc. Watch, cycle, radio, households worldly goods for son-in-law, what did his father and brothers not give to their Lado. Mother filled the nose ring, anklets, bed, rings in hand. And Sappo's hand-form was lit up with lots of bangles. Till now, Sappo, who used to flaunt in the world of the prince of her dreams, was actually understanding the meaning of marriage today. The decorations were not pleasing to her tender heart at all. The innocent bird hugging its mother was not able to leave the branch on which it was still perched.

Sappho was getting impatient by leaving away from the father's and brother's shadow and was crying loudly...."No Bapu, I don't go Don't lose my door." Day and night dreaming of the land of fairies with her prince, today she was pleading by hugging her father's feet that she should not go anywhere.

***

After coming to the city, Roshan Singh got Sappo to serve him at a Thakurani's house and got her the job of giving fodder and water to cows and buffaloes, even with a little money, his hands were free. Sappo, lost in her thoughts, was awakened from her slumber by the ringing of the door chain."Come on""Did the contractor left you early today?""Yes, give bread quickly, my body is breaking down, I am tired."Sappo, who fed bread to her husband, also finished the utensils' work quickly after eating the food. Embarrassed Sappo was blooming as if a bud was ready to burst in anticipation of a drop of dew.

***

"What's the matter, is sleeping is not coming. Tell me a few love-words, Saheb." But Saheb changed his face and turned away as if the smell of dung had put a wall between the two. She also started pretending to sleep by keeping her happiness in her fist.

The next day, Sappo could not come before her husband return."Why so late?""Nothing, there was the shaving of the ma'am's grandson. There was invitation. Feast was given to me. I will serve food for eating" Happy Sappo came to the bed after making a pot of food in her small hut."What happened over there, why are you lying with your opposite face here?"It looks like that Sappo's fate has opened, she was considering herself no less than an apsara. The scent's small vial had made a small thatched hut a palace.

***

"Don't you want to go to work today?""No, now I do not want to go to work.""Mother! send me messageLife is empty without lover. "Sappo went out in the open air humming, today she wants to become an angel and who fles in the sky.

*****

CHAPTER FIVE

SHIP BIRD

Kamla kept looking at the door again and again and sometimes at the clock on the wall. It is not known what fear is sitting in her heart that she was sweating due to nervousness even in the month of November. Husband Subodh had not returned from work. The weather was so bad as if an old war had broken out between lightning and storm. It was eleven o'clock in the night, anyway in small towns ten o'clock is midnight. The wind entered the room through the window and completely drenched Kamala, she got up slowly, changed her wet clothes, closed the window blinds and sat quietly on the chair. The storm outside had calmed down, but inside the mind, the noise was not taking the name of stopping. The clock struck twelve in the night, but there was no news of her husband so far, since the troubled sinful mind was haunted by the terror of so many unwarranted speculations.

'In what wretched moment I advised him to go to work, my useless mind was killed. Does anyone work in old age? Hey Thakur ji, now I have made a mistake, you can make up for it sometime again.' At the same time, the sound of a vehicle horn was heard, in one stroke all the chains of speculation were broken as if the speed of youth had returned, Kamala ran and opened the door before the doorbell rang."Hey, how long did you wait for me, my life was drying up? Where were you left? No news, nothing, at least call me?" "Will you keep talking in one breath or will you give me a chance to say something? The weather was bad since this evening, there was no light in the factory and I knew you would be upset, but what would you do? Seth ji did not allow his car to leave in such weather. I had gone for some work, when the car arrived, the first thing he did was to take me home." "Your seth ji is a very good man. Come on, wash your hands and face, let me serve you food."

Sudhir was sitting at the dinner table after washing his face and looking at his wife very carefully. It was felt that Kamla had not been able to get rid of the fear she had spent the last three hours in the dock. Before utensil be left from her hand, he reached out and took care of it."What are you thinking, you got upset because of such a small thing, don't think too much. Come, sit down, I will do it."Being quiet Kamla was looking for the answer to only one question.. and was mumbling...."Who does a job at this age? We will make do with whatever money Lalla sends us.""No, it's not like that, now he is also married, the expenses of the household keep on increasing and tomorrow he will have children too, we have to think about this too, then it is not right to sit empty myself at home."Your words are correct, but what should I do with my life, until you come home, my life is stuck in the throat, I neither live nor die,' Kamla said wiping her eyes."Well leave it, have food now," Sudhir said taking his wife's hand in his.

***

Sudhir Babu was very satisfied that he did a private job throughout his life and got a good education for his son with a small salary and also built a small house for his wife. The money received after retirement did not affect his son's higher education and even today his mind does not allow him to sit comfortably. Along with him, he bowed his wife's head in front of anyone. He was not ready for this at all. After the son went out for a job after higher education and got him married to a girl of his choice, the husband and wife fulfilled their responsibility with full devotion.

The son kept sending money for the expenses for many months, life was passing smoothly, but for some time some reason would have become such that it might have become his compulsion to cut the money. Thinking this, Sudhir searched for job and got job because of his old relations.Today's incident made all the equations fail. Kamla's mind was filled with such fear that she was not at all prepared for the repetition of such an incident in the future."Listen, today I got a call from Lalla, he was insisting to come there.""He does it often, it's okay! But I have to take care of myself too. Now I am tied up with my job.""So what happened, take a few days leave. Seth ji will not avoid your talk""Ok, see now go to sleep."Where is the sleep in Kamla's eyes! The sea of affection on stirring up the heart and mind with all its mightful strength."Have you gone to sleep?"When there was no answer from there, Kamla started trying to sleep by turning on the other side.

Next day Sudhir was getting ready to go to the factory."Today you will talk about holiday.""Seeing the opportunity, it is talked about for the holiday""Hey, someone's emergency can also happen""OK..OK"Sudhir interrupted his wife there with the intention of ending the matter.

Sudhir left the house for the factory but it seemed that Kamla's fearful eyes were following him. He thought, I had never seen his wife so restless before. I have been working for the whole thirty years, yes, my strength gone and must be less and now the money is also less. The money will be received according to the strength of the bone and flesh. The son said many times that both of you should come and stay here. It comes to my mind to leave everything, I also want to rest, but after listening to the wind of the world and the stories of people, my mind does not testify that I should go to my son's house and lie down in this turmoil, I do not know when the factory gate came. When I went to see, the Gorkha doorman in front of me was also looking at his face as if he was also bored with my face, his eyes are questioning about my child will definitely be unworthy. What am I thinking.

'No, I will not allow any allegation to be leveled against Aman, he takes great care of his parents.'

***

"Seth ji, I need a few days leave.""Yes, yes, you can take it whenever you want. Look Sudhir Babu, you come here for your need, not to pass the remaining time and I also cannot put a burden on my soul by making you do illegal work. You are welcome to come whenever you wish."Having said this, Sethji went away free from his charitable deed, but Sudhir Babu was left confused that 'Has Sethji really spoken about my heart or has he become relaxed by reducing any burden on his heart.' That day, Sudhir Babu did not feel like working at all, as if someone had forced a bird sitting comfortably on a tree to fly away from there. He went his home after finishing work as much as he can do till evening. Seeing her husband coming home on time, Kamla's face returned as if the brightness had disappeared. Holding a glass of water, she said..."Have you got leave?""Yes, it's a holiday, they don't have any problem.""That's it! I used to tell you that your boss is very pious."After relaxing for some time, Kamla started speaking again." I was thinking how torn your shoes are, your shoe's mouth is open from the front, you must not have noticed. I was thinking that I had to take a new shoe for yourself and a gift for my daughter-in-law and son. It is not good to go empty-handed."Sudhir Babu was thinking that wife's impatience is natural, which mother does not get restless to meet her children, my mind is also mine, few men have a heart of stone. The difference is that the woman says, but the man does not say."Tomorrow I will talk about some advance. Now you rest, I also have to rest, Aman's mother!"

**

The speed of the train had slowed down which means the platform was about to arrive. Sudhir Babu started moving forward dragging the bag with both hands."Hey, wait, let the train stop, you are getting more impatient than me."Recognized her husband's pulse Kamla spoke to him. An smile appeared on both of their faces. The happiness on their faces could not be hidden. Meeting the son was also happening after a long time.Standing on the platform, Aman greeted Babuji standing at the gate by waving his hand. As soon as the train stopped, he removed both the bags from both his hands and quickly took them off holding father's hand. Sudheer Babu helped Kamla to get down by supporting his hand. "Daughter-in-law didn't come?"Touching the feet of mother and father, Aman clarified that she had some important work in the office, so she could not come."It doesn't matter, She has to look after her job too"Malti spoke assuring herself. Seeing such a long carriage i.e. car of the son, the parents were filled with excitement and as if the chest was widened with pride. It seemed that the son had gone for a walk in the aeroplane. Came home in no time, did not know the way, the speed of the car as if the way has been shortened. The soul was pleased to see the luxuriously furnished house, both husband and wife did not forget to thank their presiding deity.

Aman showed his room to his mother and father and started making tea himself. How could mother's heart see this."My son, leave it, I will cook.""No mom, you just sit comfortably."After returning from office at night, Aman's wife went to her room after greeting her mother-in-law and father-in-law. Seeing the new era house and the way of living in that house, both husband and wife were watching everything with great curiosity and were trying to understand because they too have to adapt to this environment as long as they have to live here. Kamla couldn't believe that a shy, withdrawn girl from a small town could not believe that she was turning into something so modern. Well, she racked her brains and tried to get out of the small-town small-well frog mentality. They tried to understand it wisely. It was very good for two-three days, Aman would come from office and spend some time with his parents. The pleasure of waiting for the son and daughter-in-law to return home would have reduced the boredom of the whole day's loneliness.Son, what is your routine on Sundays?"Nothing, papa! I settle my pending work for the whole week and sometimes goes out for a walk, by the way today I have to take you out for a walk, mother will also go?" Aman asked turning to his mother."Why won't I go. Today you show your city, I should also see where my children live."

**

After coming here, everything was fine for a few weeks. After coming from Aman's office, he would go straight to his parents' room and inquire about their well-being whether they had eaten properly or not? Health is fine or not etc. etc. But gradually his busyness increased and the quota of his share of time kept decreasing.

As time passed, the children became so busy in their work that the warmth of mutual relations within them slowly started diminishing.

***

There was a strange silence at the dinner table at night, no one was talking to anyone. Son and daughter-in-law were busy with their mobiles even while having food, Sudhir Babu could not help it."My son Aman! Eat food after being relaxed""Yes Papa" Aman realized his mistake but Renu was still staring at the mobile."I want to see the schedule of tomorrow's meeting " and after finishing food quickly she started leaving the table, Aman also followed her after having food.In a new place, it takes time for a man to adapt to the formal mentality there.both husband and wife lying on their bed thinking that time has gone far ahead and how far we have left behind. It had been a month since Sudhir and Kamla had come to her son.

When the maid, who made the food went on leave for fifteen days, Kamla happily took all the burden of the house on herself. Waking up in the morning, preparing breakfast for both the children, they would have lunch in the office canteen, Kamla would prepare anything for herself and Sudhir according to their convenience and taste.

***

"Mother, put the dinner for both of us on the dining table and both of you rest after having dinner.""No Renu, nothing like that, we don't mind on it."Daughter-in-law cares so much. Kamla was heartbroken by this talk of Renu.

***

"Today you have visited the market many times, let me massage your feet."When Kamla started massaging Sudhir's feet by placing a bowl of oil on the table, Sudhir stopped her."No no Kamla, you will get rest by sleeping" but Kamla did not agree that's why Renu entered the room."Mummy, I want to talk to you about something.""Yes yes, speak daughter.""Why do you cook so much food, the food is left over and then wasted. There is some idea in mind too.""Hey, I made it for four people.""Okay then it's like this. You ask us in the evening because what happens is that often in the office everyday there is a party, it is also necessary to attend it. Well, never mind, take care in future." Saying this, Renu went to her room.

'Today Aman also went straight to his bedroom. He must be tired, he works hard all day, he needs rest.'Such a bandage of affection was tied on the eyes that on the other side the fog of insensitivity which was not visible to the old eyes was playing hide and seek with them."Listen, did you sleep?" "No, say what's the matter?" "What has happened to our Lalla?" "Hey! Nothing...they are the children of the new wind. There is a huge gap between us and their generation.""So aren't we going with them?" "The mindset of today's generation is changing very fast and the biggest thing is that the old currency was valuable in the olden times, today it is just a piece of metal, understand this thing. Now it is like this, try to sleep, don't think too much."Sudheer Babu had told his wife, but what about him too, is he too busy thinking about himself? He don't know when asleep caught sight while battling with the confusion."Papa, you dry the floor of the bathroom after bath, keep up this since wiper is there. I don't have any problem, I am saying this for the good of you people. You and mother in law are afraid of slipping and then there are slipper marks in the gallery outside too. They don't even look good." Suddenly Sudhir Babu's face fell, then he said while restraining himself.."Yes yes, you are right daughter in law, now I will take care."If Aman had said the same thing, then perhaps it would not have hurt the heart so much. Sudhir Babu was thinking that children are becoming non-existent for this house even if they do not interfere in anything, if someday they interfere, then what will happen on that day.....His mind was in turmoil, he had no choice but to comfort his heart. "It doesn't matter if the

daughter-in-law even says something. She said it for our good only"
he thought.

It had been three months since Sudhir and Kamla had come to
their son. Even if there has been some change in life after coming
here, it is a change in perception. There is a lot of difference
between the solitude here and the solitude there, the loneliness
here fills with neglectful frustrations and the loneliness there, even
after staying away from the son, the pleasant memory of the son
keeps the mind fresh and the hopes derived from his future dreams
which makes the fatigue of age meaningless. When the husband
and wife used to relive the memories related to their past days of
their son, then the feeling of happiness used to give new strength
and happiness, due to which the flame of the desire to live would
increase and with the help of that the vehicle of life could move at
a faster pace. It seemsToday the humidity of the changing season
is suffocating. It was difficult to breathe in the courtroom of
formalities. Both husband and wife get trapped in the whirlpool of
their own thoughts but do not reveal to each other.Time was taking
everyone away in its current, parallel being together, the truth of
separation was eating inside.

"Hey, did you sleep?" Kamla asked while turning her back to
Sudhir."Why... what happened? Can't you sleep?" "No, you are also
awake. Let me ask one thing, are you also thinking the same thing
that I am thinking?" Sudhir got up and sat down, more hurt by his
wife's pain than by his own pain."Yes, tomorrow I will see when the
reservation is available." "Yes, it will be fine" and Kamla also took
a sigh of relief and turned to sleep peacefully. Sudheer Babu was
gazing at Kamla's face, on whose face he was seeing deepening lines
of worry for a few days, the feeling of smooth peace was clearly
visible on that face.

*****

CHAPTER SIX

TAI JI

Taiji's mind was indecisive since this morning, she had stopped wicking lamps long ago, just one incense stick used to make her Laddu Gopal happy and Taiji used to keep looking and whispering at him for a long time, this was the daily routine, her eyes now no longer such that Ramayana or Bhagwat can be recited.

In fact, her name was Gomti, the children of the house used to call her Taiji, gradually she became Taiji of the children of the whole locality, then what was, her name Taiji became the world of children, old and young people. Even Taiji didn't know that her name Gomti, which was given by her mother-father, when and where he went missing.

She called out to her sister-in-law Anubha whom she never called by her name."Chhutki Dulhin!""Coming Jiya.""You make a bowl of porridge for me. Sister! today I do not feel like eating roti, at all.""I will make that, you don't eat something. Yesterday you get made of dumplings, but did not put even a single one in your mouth. No problem, I will make it, but you become an eater."

-------Anubha remembers that special day when Jiya's first attempt to make her the little daughter-in-law of this house and which had the warmth of a mother's loving touch which Anubha can feel even after so many years. Without a mother giving a shadow of affection to the child, the relation of Anubha's life with Gomti Devi was like that of a mother who gave birth to a son, in Anubha she looked more like a daughter than a sister-in-law.The spring blossom of Anubha's childhood had not even fully blossomed when destiny snatched her mother away from her, leaving her father and all her dreams to wander in the endless maze of life. Time runs its course and when did the vine become fit to climb the wall, the father who was struggling with the struggle of life, could not understand this.

One day Shivkumar ji, who was living in the neighborhood of Anubha's father's house, had a wedding anniversary function of his son's daughter-in-law, invitations were sent to all the houses in the neighborhood. An invitation came to Anubha's place as well and she had to go with her father despite she not wanting to. Seeing her gentle personality, Shivkumar's sister Gomti, who had come from Lucknow, was totally impressed with Anubha. Going near Anubha, she asked very intimately, placing her hand on her head, "What is your name, daughter?"Anubha had understood that she is Shivkumar uncle's sister and she is very special since everybody was respecting her. "Jee, Anubha", having said this, Anubha got up from there, being trapped in a bundle of hesitation. The matter must have come and gone, but after a few days it came to know that her brother-in-law's relation has come for her from the same aunt's house (i.e. Gomati's house). A motherless child is such a burden for her father that she considers it her duty to remove it from her shoulders even if she doesn't want to.

The day also came when she left the courtyard of her father's house and came to her in-laws' house. In-laws' family was very wealthy. Both brothers Raghuvansh and Bhagwant have an ancestral wholesale business of grocery and dry fruits in a big market. Elder brother Bhagwant's wife is Gomti Devi and they have only one son. Arvind is a brilliant student who has given his 12th examination this year and wants to pursue his further studies abroad. He is not interested in the family business. Apart from this, the ten-year-old daughter of the gardener of the house, whose name is Manno, is a very important member of this house. House's and outside's work got finished by her very quickly. The whole house is total dependent on got Manno. As soon as the morning dawns, the sweet tinkling of Manno's voice fills the whole house with supernatural peace like the Bhairavi of the dawn.

Anubha, who came after leaving her father house, saw that Aarti Parchhan was done by the hands of her sister-in-law and therefore she understood that her sister-in-law is the old woman who grew up in this house. She knew that Raghuvansh's mother had passed away four years back."Come Lala! come to the house with Lakshmi of this house." Gomti turned the hundred rupee note around the bride and the groom and handed over this note in the hands of Manno, who was standing at the door with a pot of water. Holding the note in her fist, she ran inside the house screaming and jumping. In the crowd of guests in the wedding house, Anubha was not able to understand how to start the first day in this house. After completing the rituals of Nekchar, her husband went to the meeting with his friends and she was left sitting alone on the sofa in the courtyard.

Anubha was feeling very lonely and unusual in the midst of strange house and strange people, tears were not stopping in her eyes. The memory of father kept churning inside the heart of her. An unknown fear in the mind was also not letting her take rest that some mistake might happen by her.

Bhatins sitting in the courtyard were entertaining themselves by singing song of banni-banna in their own voice and Anubha's eyes, oblivious to their dissonance, were searching for Gomti Devi.

"Come on bhauji, I will leave you to your room." When Manno started taking Anubha's hand like an old lady, a singing Bhatin interrupted her."Hey Bawri, where did you take Bahuria, let her sit in front of us.""Taiji told me to saw bhauji's room" and she quietly took Anubha's hand and took her out of that dilemma. Anubha reached the room and breathed a sigh of relief. She was suffocating wearing such a long veil since morning, Manno did that work before removing her veil from her face."Now open your face bhauji, nobody will come here. It is hot here, sit comfortably, I am going, there is some work for Taiji" and while leaving she didn't forget to turn AC on. Anubha has come to understand that this ten year old girl Manno is a very special member of this house.

Her insistent command over everyone in the house is the proof of her intimacy with this house. Gradually, Anubha also became very close to her. For her husband Raghuvansh, elder brother is like Ram. His mouth does not get tired of telling Dadda-Dadda and Dadda's wife Gomti Devi is no less than Sita Mata for him. Coming to such a beautiful and cultured family, Anubha got every happiness in the world, got the cool shade of Mamta which she had lost in her childhood.

Coming to her in-laws house, the pure love of her sister-in-law had filled the emptiness in her life due to the departure of her mother. Jeth ji (brother-in-law), a man of serious, cultured saintly attitude, used to speak less but whatever he speak, he used to speak logically and ethically. No one in the house had the courage to cut his words. He was not interested in the family business with which destiny had connected him, but his sense of duty always took him to the same path of work on which he did not want to walk. Responsibility towards his better half would also leave him at times. Everyone was unaware of the script that the supreme god was writing. There was a son Arvind, he wanted to become an engineer after studying, he also wanted to settle abroad like his friends. There was only one younger brother, Raghuvansh, on whose shoulders the burden of the ancestral business was placed.

"Aunt, you are well educated, tell my father that I want to study abroad" Arvind used to persuade aunt with great love and ask her to recommend him, because he knew that no one would avoid aunt's words."Yes, I will talk. Right now your holidays are going on. Go and sit at the shop for some time. See, your father and uncle will also glad to see it" Anubha explained to him. But everyone was defeated in front of the child's stubbornness and Arvind was sent to study abroad. Here Bhagwant also used to sit less at the shop, spend more time in worship or would go to some satsang and return home after hours. Seeing the change in her husband, Gomti Devi was distraught."Listen, what is your attitude? Forgetting the attention of your home, which way did you go? Right now I am sitting, when I pass away, you do whatever you want."Bhagwant didn't say anything after listening to his wife, he just used to smile. Later it came to know from someone that a Siddha Mahatma had come to the ashram on the banks of the river, where he had taken initiation from him.Gradually, his distaste for his wife and family became apparent to everyone.

"Dad, what are we listening to. Do you know the meaning of initiation? You are forgetting the direction of the house and my bhauji's face. Even Arvind is not here, what should I see alone. At least think about bhauji.""Hey Chutkau, you are here, Dulhin is here, so why I will be worried about this? Brother! My mind is very upset. It's all destiny's work, no one can do anything about it."

Then one day such a dawn came which stamped everything which Bhagwant Babu had said. Another night, another Siddhartha of Kali Yuga left home and freed his Yashodhara from every bondage. After a long time someone told that he had gone to Nepal, someone said that he had seen him in Kolkata in saffron clothes. All persons have their own words, but Gomti Devi was discharging her duties more faithfully in her small family, which was her work place. After going in search of peace of her husband, she was calming down herself. She does not want this sacrifice of her husband to embarrass her or her husband. Beyond everyone's sympathy, that self-respecting woman was always ready to raise her head proudly and carry her own burden as well as the burden of others.

One day Jiya was a little bit too silent, after completing the household works, Anubha came and sat next to Jiya."Jiya! what are you thinking?""Nothing, Dulhin! What I will think? Whom I were thinking, is now got freed from world" saying this, her throat filled with tears, but seeing her morale breaking in front of someone, she calmed down as if she was about to commit a mistake.

Till now, Anubha has seen Jiya brimming with confidence, keeping every brick and every utensil of the house safely locked in the fist of her responsibility. If someone's eye twitches or hangs in the house, anywhere in any corner, Jiya has a panacea for every sorrow, then why has Jiya been compensating for the irresponsible step of her husband, neglecting her health? It was beyond understanding and in such a situation, Anubha's head would have bowed further with respect towards Jiya and she would have taken her hand in hers and tried to remove herself and all her sorrows.

--Gomti Devi vs Taiji's sister-in-law Anubha, the daughter of an educated cultured family used to respect her sister-in-law like her mother and used to address her as Jiya. For a few days Anubha was observing that after getting a slight hint of Taiji's eyes, the cycle of activities of the whole house either stops or starts running at double the speed, the same Taiji now often has a mist of noiseless desolation in the eyes, lays on her bed silently staring at the ceiling. Till now, Taiji used to stand as a shield in every kind of ups and downs in the family or relations and after husband Bhagwant left home, time had made her even stronger. Everyone considered himself lucky. Her purpose of keeping the whole household balanced and safe from trouble was what gave her strength.

-------Today, Anubha was thinking that Jiya, who satisfies others and fills her stomach with only two morsels, is asking for something to eat for the first time, so she quickly made porridge and brought it.

"Hey, have you worn the same pink saree again today, many times I have told you that this saree has become old, now why you not retire it? This would be used in the work of making chips and papad. Dozens of sarees are stored in the chest, what about them? Wear them all, I thinj you have a lot of attachment to this saree.""Hey, you are speaking in one breath, Chhutki! whether you want to give time to me to speak something?"

After pausing for a while, Taiji spoke again,"What do you say, Dulhin! why is there no attachment to it? Your Jeth ji had brought it on the wedding anniversary and did you know, for the first time on that day, my mind was blinking? it was your Jethji's saree, I would have worn the same thing given and I have not spoken anything to him."

Anubha asked seeing her voice slowing down..."Jiya! are you sleeping?" "Why don't you let us stay quietly, Dulhin?" Taiji got annoyed as if the straws of the bygone days have drifted in the lake of her eyes.

---"Hey, Badki! today you are blooming like a lotus flower?" Don't know, what do you want to say?" The pink colored saree had given more brightness to the pink color of Taiji's round cheeked cheeks. Out of shame, she went inside that what would anybody say if someone hears it. It is felt very good but Taiji was mumbling, "hey, what has happened with you? Old age has come but youth is felt."

Today Jia slept without any reason, she would have put something in her stomach. What are she mumbling, it looks like she is dreaming."Jiya! wake up, let's eat only a little porridge, it is too late, today you have asked for porridge after a long day." "Why don't you wake up, Jiya?"

Jiya would get up if she would be there, she was sitting ready since morning wearing a pink saree to go on her last journey.

*****

CHAPTER SEVEN

LIFE'S DUSK

It was the month of December, Sudha sat in the sun after finishing all the household chores.

Today there was not so much sunlight in the balcony as strong wind was blowing. Even though there was a slight mist of fog, yet a little bit of sunshine felt good. After sending Manoj to the office, Sudha felt a bit relaxed, at the same time she used to think about herself, something about the future. Sudha was interested in reading since childhood, so within two years of marriage, she had made a good collection of books like her maternal home. This was her addiction which she could not leave. The companian of mother-in-law left within a year of her marriage. She had suddenly died of a heart attack. After her departure, there was utter loneliness, when Manoj used to go to office at nine o'clock, then these books were the companion of Sudha's loneliness. Sudha was lost in some thoughts that the doorbell rang, went and saw Radha aunty standing.Sudha: "Hey Aunty you!?"Radha: "Yes daughter-in-law! I wanted to meet you guys, so I came here."Sudha: "Well done, you must be tired, it is so cold, let's sit in the sun."Sudha grabbed the bag from Radha's hand and brought her inside.Sudha: "Aunt! tell me more, how is everyone at home? Is everyone fine?"Radha: "Yes daughter! Everyone is fine. Now you will give me hot tea first or will you keep talking?"

Sudha brought her aunt to the same room where her mother-in-law used to live.Malti, The mother-in-law of Sudha, and Radha were sisters in far off relationship. But both were friend with respect to relationship. Last year when friend (Malti) had passed away, she had come to Delhi and had gone back after her13th. Sudha was thinking how much aunt has changed in one year. The lines on the face are horizontal, the complexion is dark and it has become subdued, still there was a soft smile on the face. Still, Sudha seemed to know why this smile was hiding a lot. Sudha brought tea after making it, suddenly there was silence in the room. Malti's photo was pasted on the wall. When Sudha saw her aunt wiping her eyes, she hesitated and started opening her bag.Radha: "See how is this, daughter-in-law?"There was the cloth of a suit was of light sky color. Sudha was elated to see this where the silk embroidery work being done.Sudha: "Very beautiful aunt but what was the need of it."Radha: "Look at Manoj's shirt cloth and tell me how it is?"Sudha: "It is very good aunt, I am missing mother-in-law a lot today."Radha: "Yes daughter, it is only the memory of her that has pulled me here. I thought, otherwise what happened, she has children, I will go there and cool my chest."Sudha:" You have done well."Radha: "Me and Malti were more friends than sisters since childhood. We may not have been together in each other's happiness, but we were companions in every sorrow, she has gone, I don't know how many more days I have to live, when I will be called by the god."Sudha: 'Why are you saying this, you are not alone, your son is Ravi and we are also your children." Radha began to caress Sudha's head lovingly. Sudha also felt as if the lack of mother-in-law's love, which she used to feel day and night after her departure, has been fulfilled today. After Manoj came from the office in the evening, the conversation continued for a long time, only Malti as if everyone was consoling each other by expressing their feelings.It didn't even know how a week passed. One day when Sudha went to Radha Aunt's room to give her tea, Radha aunt was sitting with her bag ready.Sudha: "What happened, what is all this, you have kept all the things, you have put your bag, where are you going?"Radha: "I am just going. I am happy to have met you people, now I will leave. Children must be waiting for me. The daughter-in-law will say that she sat there and completely forgot us."Sudha: "That's fine aunty, you would have stayed for one or two more days, I was feeling so good with you."Radha: "No problem daughter, I will come again, what is mine, picked up the bag and left. No one is going to stop me, I am the master of my own will, and Modinagar is not far from Delhi, then I will come again."

Manoj had gone on tour outside the city, he was also not at home, Sudha was thinking again the same loneliness. May be he had to come back till today evening, he had said so. Sudha has feeded breakfast to Radha aunty and she tried to keep some gifts for the children.Radha: " What is you keeping daughter? No, no, whenever they will come, you give these to them" saying this she put both packets back on the bed.Radha: "Now you will do something and by making me a rickshaw to the bus stand."

Sudha reluctantly got down and came upstairs after making aunt sit on the rickshaw. It seemed as if the house was more desolated than before. Sudha sat on the sofa, then what happened to her mind that she went to mother-in-law's room and sat on the bed, suddenly she saw a diary near the pillow and started thinking, oh, this is aunt's diary, maybe it was left outside while packing the bag. The accounting book was also written. Sudha thought that it was unethical to see someone's diary like this, but she thought that she should call her aunt's son Ravi and tell him that her aunt is gone and only one diary is left. After seeing she has got Ravi's phone number. A long time ring has gone but nobody picked up. Again she rang, then from another side one lady's voice came.

Sudha: "Hello who? Who is calling from Ravi brother's place?"From there the answer came in 'yes' I am his wife Rekha speaking. Sudha said I have made my aunt sit at the bus stand but one of her diary is left here, I thought I will tell you, when aunt will come you will tell her.Rekha: "Look, it's like mother-in-law doesn't live with us. It has been four years since she left home, she has been living in Nari Niketan for the last four years. I don't even have her phone number, maybe my husband has it, I will tell him in the evening. At this time he is not at home."

If it is cut, there is no blood, Sudha's understanding replied. She wishes, if mother-in-law were present at this time, it would be something different. Sudha rolled on the bed and started crying bitterly saying "why do people do this?" Dusk was also starting to descend in the courtyard, the mind started sinking in even more sadness. It had been heard that the evening of life is very long, it does not get cut. She started waiting for Manoj very willingly.

*****

CHAPTER EIGHT

WILD HERB

At this time, it is early morning, yet there is a slight interference of darkness in the valleys of the forest. The forest wealth spread far and wide, flaunting mangoes, mahoba and dense densed Peepal and Neem trees, from which a little light is coming, as if a bride is playing a game of hide and seek, dressed as a lover.

Chaitali eyes opened early in the morning today and then she came in the forest to pick up wood. She was carrying the burden of a bundle of dry wood and bamboo splinters on her head, but carrying the burden of being barren on her chest, at this time she was thinking that 'I wish I would be blessed with a child in my heart', the wind whirling between the trees was burning more fire than cold in her body. Today she was not at all inclined to go ahead. Earlier, whenever the mind was indecisive, she would not stay at home for a moment and would go far in search of herbs in this rugged forest; Sometimes she would have earned some money by selling herbs, but today the fearless madness of the mind wants something else.

The sorceress of the forest wielded such a magic wand that Chaitali began to let down the bundle of wood right there in the soil. The hypnosis of the dew-drenched soil of the night, the hypnosis of the sweet smell of Mahua's trees tied her feet and her body spread like a river and her heart started sinking in the boat of those golden dreams which were far away from her life."Hey, what do you do here, Chaita?"Faguniya shook Chaitali so tightly that she sat up in fear."Oye! What would have done, Badki? You have broken my golden dream.""There old woman is shouting guns of unwanted words and here you sleeping."Tearing eyes at her sister-in-law, she got up and left."Would you not want to burn oven, now ? When Faguniya interrupted again, Chaitali realized that she had forgotten the bundle of wood she had collected.'Now a days, no work is good, but I don't know every now and then where I will get lost, have I become dizzy?' Chaita bubbled in the mouth.

The elusive world of the forest, in which the rustling wind hums in a slow tone, the intoxicating fragrance of green trees was the world of dreams of Chaita, when she used to come out of the house on the pretext of picking wood when she was sad. Just as she had fallen in love with the gray darkness of the dense forest, she used to enjoy playing with colorful wild birds. Just sixteen years old, Chaita was married to a boy who was older than her but younger in intelligence. As cool as Chaita, he was equally pundit and coward that father mother named son as Pelu. With father Makru, he used to go to work as an agricultural labourer. Both the father and son would have earned so much that the bread and pulses of the house would have come out. Mother Shanichari used to coddle Pelu, her step-son, but not as much as she used to pamper her own son Saravan, she would never hurt him, but whenever she saw Pelu, she would remember her mother Sugna, whose bite she has not forgotten till date.

**

"Who is she? Who is she with you , who is turning around me?"Seeing a stranger girl with Makru, Shanichari could not help but ask."This Sugna now live here." Makru just gave a short answer, didn't tell much, lest Shanichari create a ruckus. For a few days, Makru had started going across the line for farming wages, where he met Sugna and while working together, both fell in love. Sugna was enraged by the enthusiasm of youth and young Makru, so Makru also lost heart on Sugna. Both of them performed the ritual of filling vermilion in the temple and became husband and wife. When Shanichari saw both of them and seeing whitening vermilion on the head of Sugna, Shanichari ascended to the sky with anger."Will you get married with her?" "Yes, just understand this." "You both should hold the whole stitch of stone on my chest."Makru sat silently as he knew it was better to remain silent at this time. Carrying her two-year-old son Saravan in her arms, Shanichari came out stomping her feet. For a few days, there were daily quarrels in the house. Sugna used to silently tolerate Shanichari's taunts day and night because she loved Makru very much. Time passed like this and Shanichari's anger cooled down like the boiling of stale curry. Within a year, Sugna became pregnant and she had to walk to serve Sugna even against her will. Shanichari's taunts on every words and a sense of guilt took her life. One day Sugna, a victim of TB, left the world forever by putting Pelu in Shanichari's lap. Shanichari accepted Pelu as the law of destiny, but half-heartedly anyway, no matter how much the stepmother loves, when it comes to dividing the share between step child and own child, she definitely does a little bit of dishonesty, be it love or any other thing. Shanichari was also in the same condition, that is why Pelu, weak in body and dull-witted, was neither able to stand on his feet properly nor be a part of anyone's love in the house. Chaita had understood that Saravan's place in the house does not belong to her man, due to which she used to face a lot of trouble. For the respect of her husband, she would rush with anyone and would always stand in front of him as a shield, but that innocent man could never understand this. The bigger the heart of a woman, the deeper is the ocean of her feelings. Husband's love touch yearning woman gradually creates such a world within herself and the mirage of her imagination which not only keeps her life alive but also keeps her life from going astray by making it directionless.

**

One day Pelu returned to total tired in the evening and after eating bread, lay down on the cot lying in the shed and fell asleep in a deep sleep. When Shanichari saw him, she told shaking his body, Why did you turn from son?What happened? Isn't there something to tell me?"Pelu went to his herd without saying anything.Going inside meant that it was beyond the mind of Pelu, he would go to sleep quietly and Shanichari would not desist from peeping, and thats why he could not stop for a day.....''Did you turn dead? Are you lying in the dust of the soil. Are you not seeing that your husband had come?''Chaita immediately got up after hearing her mother-in-law's voice. Kill her mind, the poison she has been drinking till now.The old woman, who was unaware of her pain, had nothing to do with it. She would have gone out by showing the matchstick to the fire of the body but would have left the Chaita to die in the cold of the cold sea.Many months have passed, then years have passed, now Shanichari has woken up from her sleep. Something is fishy.Chaita's heart kept peeling with her sweet knife and caressing son Pelu with her folded belly with a bandage on her eyes.

While treating the people of her community with herbs, Shanichari had become a half-doctor. Gradually, clever woman came to know whether the deficiency was in the field or in the seed. She would feed both of them by bringing herbs from the forest and keep a sharp eye on both of them, especially every month she would keep an eye on Chaita. Sometimes a lamp lit by the village deity at the door, if someone had told her to blow it, she would have done it too, but the womb of Chaita was lying like a barren land and has not turned green yet.

**

Shanichari's sharp eyes were always on Chaita. One day she came from the forest and she was standing that what she saw the raw mangoes tied in her cover, mountains of speculation started touching the sky in her mind.''Hey son! Why do you want to eat tart? For which purpose this mango?'' ''No, mother! This is for sister in law. She told me for this.''

She didn't agree without asking with a suppressed tongue.''Why did you turn to take a bath every month, didn't you?''Shrinking like thieves when Chaita said..''Yes, mother'', so it didn't take long for his attitude to change.

''All infertiles dragged everythings on my chest'', saying this, she went out grumbling.

**

Elder son Saravan, a truck driver, often used to stay out of the house in order to carry goods from the village to the city. When he came home in ten days or in a week, the whole house would have been overwhelmed by seeing him. Shanichari and Phaguniya would have celebrated Diwali only. He would bring something or the other for everyone, such as studded tikuli, meenedar bangles, flowered ghagra-choli etc. He would open the gift box after coming from the city"Look, mother! I have come with the most expensive ghagra for you, now show me wearing it" Shanichari's arms blossomed immediately, she would have cast a cursory glance at Faguniya, puffed up with the pride of her mother, Shanichari's face would have been full of pride. She would have taken a quick look at Fagunia immediately. Full of pride in her mother, Shanichari's face would run with arrogant redness. Faguniya sitting in the corner was watching every piece when her lover would give her some gift too. After pleasing his mother, taking Faguniya with him, he enters his tart or hut and does not pass out for hours. He would have shut mother's mouth in advance by giving her colorful bangles and ghagras, and she too would have swelled up after getting all this and all the others would have gone ignoring the closed door by her force and would have said, "your house this is, and you better know." That proud woman would go away holding the hand of one of the two daughters of Phaguniya and carrying the other in her arms.This time Faguniya had started to suspect something had changed since Saravan had come home."You don't look at me, neither you care about me, it is not known, to whom with you are? It seems you are not loving me", Faguniya, who was lightheaded because of her pregnancy, could not muster the courage to ask him anything. Saravan went out after eating roti and returned home drunk late at night.Spreading a cot in the porch, Saravan lay down there and continued to blow his beedi. This time, as he did not have time to see his wife. Fire started burning in her body, but she could not do anything.' O God, when will he go back to the city, I can breathe in peace, he is ready to raise his hands on me if I say something.Day by day the same excesses are increasing. The old woman shuts her mouth if she doesn't care about any complaint." "You are a man, you are not a woman who will wear bangles and sit down. Whatever comes in mind ask from Mora", but Faguniya didn't get courage to ask. Chaita sees the sorrow of her sister-in-law but is unable to do anything and then the mother-in-law finds it difficult to sit together with both of them, she separates both of them on one pretext or the other and keeps one in her court.This time Faguniya was seven months pregnant and every day Shanichari used to pray to one or the other deity with folded hands. ' If you turn the grandson this time, I will accept your request to offer eleven kilos of laddus to Vanadevi.'But destiny had something else in store for Shanichari'sgrandson happiness was not written in her fate, she gave birth prematurely in the eighth month, but this time also a girl child was born, that too dead, turning water on all the hopes.There was mourning in the house, but the old woman still did not lose courage, in the hope of her grandson, her eyes were now fixed on Chaita, like the eyes of a chatak look towards the sky waiting for the nectar drops of rain.

**

Today Chaita's heart was very sad, she could not sleep. She placed her hand on Pelu's chest as if giving a silent message to his body and mind, and she wants to drench him with love. The night kept on deepening and the unseen sweet hangover of love kept on wobbling within the four walls, she kept searching for herlover in this search, even her unseen dreams could not know when Chaita's eyes fell.

Pelu had left for work with his father before Chaita woke up very late in the morning. When she went to the kitchen, she saw that the pulse, kept on the stove, was about to start burning and Faguniya was sitting holding her head lost in her own thoughts. Faguniya woke up from sleep as soon as she heard "Where are your attentions, Faguniya all pulses have become coal". "Hey mother! my foolness may be fired on" pulling out the wood from the stove and sat down she was crying. To suppress the fear of Shanichari,

Faguniya started cursing and abusing herself.By the way Saravan had gone to the city for a month ago and there was no news. When living in the village, Faguniya used to be beaten up, she used to persuade him to return to the city as soon as possible and now when there was no news about him for so many days, the wretched untoward incident was not letting her to rest.

**

"Everyone's bread and water have been arranged. Why are you sitting here? You go and take rest."Shanichari said lovingly caressing Chaita's head. Longing for mother-in-law's love, Chaita got drenched with love and her eyes filled with tears. For the first time, she got to hear such pampering words from mother-in-law's mouth. When she went to her tart, the mother-in-law closed the door. As soon as she entered the closet, a strange foreign smell entered Chaita's nose like a colic. She could understand something that in the blink of an eye, the tart became dark. Before the darkness outside made its way inside and before the fire of the body which she had been saving within herself for years in the hope of light, this night, she ran outside screaming, saving herself from the savage burning."Save me."Her screams may or may not have been heard by someone else, Pelu heard her bragging and ran towards the tart. Pelu was standing outside the door with embers of anger in his eyes, with a pole ex in his hand. Today, seeing Pelu face to face in front of her, could not believe it for a moment and like a half-opened vine, she went and hugged him.

"Don't leave him. Darken his face, this mortals' man."Pelu went inside and pulled Saravan out. Today destiny was with Chaita, the invisible power of her love had awakened Pelu's masculinity and forced him to stand on the threshold of duty. Freed from the ghost of untowardness, Chaita wanted to forget every fear by getting into Pelu's chest because her wait was over today.

*****

CHAPTER NINE

COMEBACK

An insulting reprimand, only a bitter attitude suddenly takes everything away with it, in its inundation. Years ago, the time spent with loved ones, the linked links of relationships, which everyone keeps like a heritage. But what an irony it is that the good and happiness-giving things get washed away somewhere and what remains is the pain of unpleasant moments, which remains like sediment. Who knows more than Malti how difficult it is to breathe amidst that sediment.

For some time she sat bewildered, don't know how many questions were running in her mind."Why?" "For why?" "And for how long?", "Why? " "For whom?" and "How long can this go on?"It is not known when she went into the lap of sleep like a fluttering sparrow imprisoned in the cage of questions.

When she opened her eyes in the morning, she saw that the sun was blooming outside, the clouds had dispersed. Seeing the sun, the depression of the mind also got relieved, she got some relief. The scorching sun felt good by her after the thunder storm and raining ammunition in the night and her mind was also quiet.

Malti quickly got up and retired from her routine and reached the kitchen and she saw that Kalpana and her mother was busy with preparing breakfast."I am late in getting up sister-in-law, now give me, I will cook it." Kalpana's mother intercepted the matter."It's okay now, are you feeling fine my daughter?"The taste of Malti's mouth became astringent after listening to the loving address from

Aunty's mouth, yet she said laughing, "yes ok aunty, I slept very late at night that's why I opened my eyes late."Ajit was waiting for breakfast in the meeting hall outside."Hey, how long will it take? I have to leave early, there is an urgent meeting in the office, hurry up.""Yes, just bringing it," Kalpana replied from the kitchen."Bring it sister-in-law, I will take it.""Yes, yes, sister you take this sandwich, I will bring more."When Malti came out with Ajit's breakfast, Ajit's eyes fell on Didi, but as if he could not meet eye with her."Forgive me sister for the talk of the night, you may have felt bad, I did not intend to hurt you at all.""No, no, brother! no problem, you have breakfast, it's getting late." Saying this, Malti went to her room. What the room! The room was a store where old boxes, almirahs were kept. There was an old iron rack next to it, in which waste material collected over the years, scraps of old newspapers, a mixer grinder etc were waiting to go to the scrapyard. An almirah was kept, a diwan was lying on the support of the wall. In this room, there was a picture of mother and father on the front wall. Many times her heart wanted to put the picture of Dev on the wall, so that the pain of loneliness would be less, but due to hesitation, she could not muster the courage to do so. Although the image of the beloved one never disappears from the eyes, but there comes a moment when the wall of restraint begins to crack and Malti takes out Dev's photo from her almirah and talks to him, she feels as if she is in the company of her husband. The shadow of sanjeevan used to breathe life into the inert body for some time and remove all the suffering and Malti would then go on for the journey ahead, but last night's incident struck like lightning on all possibilities of relations. The walls of love and trust collapsed and she was left standing at the crossroads like a homeless person.

There was a place for worshiping God in one corner. Because of this, Malti never wanted to go away from this room, whenever she was in sad, she used to talk to her presiding deity. But today the mind was getting disenchanted with her too, the misty whirlwind of the past bent on taking her away from the present.

***

"Dev , when will this painting work be finished? Tell the contractor to finish it soon, he said for fifteen days, one month is coming.""Yes, I will tell Baljeet, he will make boost his boys, it will happen soon."That's it, Avi's final exams are coming, without arranged home, no work is done properly. Child's education is being lost, Dev !"

Dev and Malti had built their dream home with great love. Every wall of the house was painted with love and security and heavenly amenities added to the elegance of life.A gift given by God, a promising son, well-mannered with intelligence, like a wave of affection that makes parents proud. When the child is promising, parents start dreaming about their children, the height they could not reach, they want to make their child higher than themselves and they want to see at the peak of their children. Same thing happened with Avi. Sending abroad for higher education broadens the chest with pride, but it also gives the pain of being away from their children, but every parent bears that pain happily by keeping a stone on their heart and they don't even say 'oops'. A person does work with extreme self-confidence but he is unable to read the lines written on his forehead that through which turns he will pass through the path that destiny has chosen for him. Dev died in a road accident, Malti's life started wandering like a straw caught in a storm and this wandering came to the fore as a cruel irony of life."Mom, you come with me to America.""No son, your studies are not even completed yet, now you have to focus only and only on your goal. When you will get job, I will go with you myself."Avi was left heartbroken and went back with a half heart.

**

Did I make a mistake at that time, was my decision wrong that I did not go to America with my son, Malti got entangled in the question and trying to reconcile the scattered straws of life, she started pacifying herself.Not because of her stubbornness, but there were many reasons because of which she did not go to America with her son, she refused thinking that she cannot live so far across seven seas. All my loved ones are here, the soil here where I was born, my childhood, my workplace, sweet memories of intimate time spent with my husband after marriage, everything is here.It was her wish that her soil should be found in the soil of her land. She was paying a very heavy price for this desire, but at last night Ajit's talk broke her heart, as if a boatman has left the boat stuck in the mid-stream to drown in the whirlpool and sat down on the shore. She tried a lot so that there should not be a rift in the relationship between brother and sister, she kept on forgiving her mistakes again and again, but today the tide of anger was trying to test its speed, Malti was trying to save the dam somehow. It should not break, otherwise it will be her own defeat.The script was being written elsewhere, the characters were playing their parts as puppets, unaware of each other's state of mind.The next day the door of Malti's room was locked."Look, even today your sister-in-law quin will make an excuse."After listening to her mother, Kalpana thought, "Let me see why didi has not come today down till now." When she saw the door was not locked, it opened as soon as she touched it. All the furniture in the room was in its place, but Malti was not there, instead her letter was testifying to her absence.

"Dear brother Ajit, you are younger than me, that's why I kept taking your name, but after father's departure, I started feeling that you are father's successor, so I made you humanly sit at the same place, I don't know whether I did right or wrong. After passing away my husband you have taken a lot of care of me and my son Avi. Ajit! I felt like my brother is with me then I will win every battle of life. This mirage of mine kept increasing day by day, I used to expect more and more from you which was wrong and I should not have done. Today I am realizing that. I did not accept to go with my son, it was my right or wrong decision. At that time I came to this house with you on your insistence, unaware of the answer to these questions. Then I started feeling proud of my brother, but brother, crossing any boundary is wrong, be it on the ground of emotions or in physical life. Today I feel that my decision taken so many years ago has affected Avi and myself. I have done injustice with myself but I have also done injustice to you. Whatever happened yesterday turned out to be okay, it showed my vision a new path. Yesterday you, sister-in-law and her mother were talking to each other, then some sounds fell in my ears too. Forgive me.

****

"When your sister has a house, why doesn't she live there?""Mother, I have told him so many times, but he is fond of becoming great, isn't he? Due to him, we husband and wife also quarrel. What should I do, we also need a little privacy, mother! But he doesn't understand this." "My son Ajit! Kalpana is telling right." Kalpana's mother put another match. Ajit shouted loudly."Will you all let me live or not?" It seemed as if some spark was smoldering inside Ajit for many days, today it flared up as soon as it got air."I am fed up with all these things, leave me alone, everyone go away from here!" Ajit shouted very loudly.The excess of helplessness was sitting behind the sharpness of the voice. Malti could not bear hearing such a loud voice of Ajit."What happened Ajit, are you fine brother?""Why do you keep listening to us secretly. Nothing happened, I am fine, you go from here."As soon as one stitch of the seam breaks, the whole seam starts opening. Malti did not want that once the seam of the relationship opened, it would continue to open again, she would not allow this to happen.

**

"Hello, Baljeet!"

"Yes madam?"

"I am speaking Malti from Dev Niwas"

"Yes ma'am! Please speak."

"Baljit! You have to come tomorrow sometime to fix the house, it was closed for many years."

*****

CHAPTER TEN

PLATFORM OF NEEM-TREE

This morning he got up before sunrise. The mind was very happy, the day started well. One eye was opened on that time, otherwise, he is in the greed of sleeping more on a holiday. On holiday, he lies in bed till 10 o'clock, then after that the shadow of kofta would surround him like a ghost and destroy all the freshness of the whole day.

He was thinking that today his almirah should be tidied up. When his wife goes to her maternal home, he likes to fly like a free bird as per his wish. He eats and drinks according to his own way, having fun like a bachelor has its own fun.

Even now humming the song, while taking bath under the shower in the bathroom, was giving him the great pleasure of kingship. His heart wished that he should keep taking bath like this, and kept on singing without any hindrance, exact at that time the phone's ringing made everything go gurgle."Hello.""Yeah, what are you doing, dear?" His wife's voice came from another side."What do you do? I am taking a bath, why are asking? is there any problem?""No, I thought you were sleeping. I am to wake you up.""No, I got up early today.""Okay, let's talk later."

Wife, Suman, put down her phone. He also came out of the bathroom and entered the kitchen to make his breakfast. After having breakfast, he thought that his wardrobe should be fixed.

So while rummaging through the old papers, old black and white photos were found, and his eyes got stuck on the one in which his entire family of ten people are there. Grandfather with a big mustache like a captain in the middle, grandmother next to him, four sons (of his grandfather) with their wives sitting around them. Downstairs, he is also sitting on the second number in the group of six children. Joint family has its own happiness. Suddenly his gaze got stuck on elder uncle's face, on his severed nose. He remembered that his Babujee used to narrate big stories about the bravery of Taujee. He had a lot of status. He was a landowner. A magnificent Bagghi would always stand at the door of the house. If the ladies of the house had to go somewhere, they used to sit in it. But when elder Taujee had to go to other villages for recovery, he used to go on his horse. It is said that once he went out for recovery, it was night and on the way he got lost in the forest, till far there was no trace of any human caste. Yes, he did encounter a ghost. Seeing the ghost, the horse was startled and Taujee fell on the ground with a thud. Due to this, his nose was broken, and taking the name of Bajrangbali with the injured nose, somehow saved his life and ran backwards. The wound was so deep that the shape of the nose itself changed. When he came home and told this story, some people did not believe him and made fun of him, while some thanked the almighty that he had come back home safely. Today, after seeing the photo, he remembered everything, but today he could not believe it. It was rather a laugh that it was all nonsense. It was already afternoon. The stomach rats had also started making a ruckus in the stomach and he entered the kitchen to make something.

He didn't like to spend the whole day cooking in the kitchen like women, so to end the boredom, he went outside to take dinner. When he was returning after eating, he found Miss Rosie, the owner of the house at the main gate, who did not like her eyes."Oye Man! Now-a-days you are alone. If any problem, you tell me.""O! Yes Aunty."Miss Rosie is a retired old lady. Very superstitious and short-tempered. Whenever she came in front, he would have cut the cane and left, but today it happened face to face.

Rosie Aunty has put an iron gate in the middle of the common gallery of both the houses, in which she keeps it locked and whenever she opens, she drips like unseasonal rain, but she has given strict instructions not to close it from here.

He is very annoyed with his house owner because of many small things like this.After coming, he lay down on the bed to get up early in the morning. Don't know where will have to go for reporting tomorrow.--------------Today he has to go to Alipura for news covering. The strike is going on in the sugar mill there. The situation has worsened due to the clash between the two factions divided between the factory owner and the union. It is said that a man has died. He took his other companion Sultan along. The distance from his office to the village would be forty kilometres. Both left on the bike.

Today, due to reaching on time on duty, he could not even have breakfast, had just left home after having a cup of tea and biscuits, so it was natural for stomach rats to jump in his stomach."Friend Sultan! if you see any dhaba or tea shop, stop it. Let's eat and drink something and then go ahead" But Sultan did not agree.

"Now the village is about to come. Look, the boundary of the village has started."The month of May was so hot that even the water bottle was over as if heat waves were raining from the sky. Only then a paan-beedi shop appeared in a small pond on the side of the road."Stop-stop."He got down from the motorcycle and brought a bottle of water. The name was written as Bisleri, but its printing was telling that it is fake Bisleri, but where does heat and thirst see all this. He asks for water and he drank half the bottle with his gusto.

"What a time. People lose their faith even for something like water"A little further ahead, a Neem-tree and its platform were seen, then Sultan stopped the bike and both of them sat on that platform to rest. There was also a well next to the platform, on whose pulley a rope was mounted, and a bucket was also placed below to fill water. Now both of them were sitting that only then a stout man passed by on a bicycle."Why are you sitting here?

Don't know, sitting here is forbidden.""First tell us, whether will I get some foods and drinks here?""There is no stuff here.. go back on reverse feet, and yes don't even touch this well""Why brother, what's the matter, is there a ghost here?" He said mockingly at him."Yes, not one here! Two ghosts live here.""Hey! Are you kidding, I just said it in jest""But I'm not kidding. If you love your life, get out of here."Educated urban people don't believe the words of others quickly. They also don't take the words of the people of village seriously.

He and his companion laughed out loud."Tell us exactly which ghost has camped here.""What will you do after knowing? This is not a matter of dillygay, measure your way""Yes, yes, will go but tell us right you don't want your name to appear in tomorrow's newspaper? We are newspapermen.""It was a long time ago, once a year, a fair of Mata used to be held in this village. People from distant villages used to come to the fair carrying their goods in bullock carts. Once upon a time, Kunwarpal's clan came to the fair with his 10-20 family members and stayed at this neem-tree platform. Here on the other side of the well, he dug the ground with spade and sickle and tied a chholdari for his living and started living comfortably. Wooden toys, bamboo etc, they made a living by making colorful baskets and selling them in the fair. There was a young girl named Jhumri in that nomadic tribe. Unfortunately, a boy from the village named Ballu fell in love with her. Jhumri also loved Ballu very much. Kunwarpal, the head of the clan, was unhappy with this. He put guards on the girl. But both the lovers kept meeting secretly. Even the villagers did not like this thing. The boy of their village married a girl of a different caste and kept the relationship. In the midst of the fair, there were a lot of fights and lathis, then suddenly something happened that the neem platform became empty overnight and from that day Ballu also went missing. A lot of searching was done but Ballu was nowhere to be found.

The next year, when the fair was held, some people of the nomadic tribe saw the shadow of two ghosts roaming around the well at night. But the people of the village did not believe this. The fair was not even full that the fire broke out on the second day of the fair. People began to have an illusion that it may or may not be the wrath of evil spirits. But the contractor of the fair, who was the surveyor of the fair also, did not listen to the people."I didn't keep anything in these things, the fair will go on like this, today I will be careful, I will watch all night."What happened that night that the dead body of the contractor was found near the well in the morning.Since then the fair has also stopped in this village and no one even turns here.""When no one comes and goes here, then why is there a rope and a bucket to fill water here?""This is the secret, no one knows. Everyone says that both lovers live somewhere here. You also run away from here." It was night while talking to that stranger. Both forgot hunger and thirst in his words.

"What to do now, the work for which we had come, that too was not done. Looks like the job is gone" he muttered with trembling lips."You are in need of a job, here you are in love"When the Sultan started the bike quickly..."Is this, what the tire puncture was supposed to happen now!"

When he looked back at the deserted place on a dark moonless night, even the cyclist could not be seen far away. The mind was numb and there was no way to get out of the silence like a forest. There is no sign of habitation in the distance, not even the twinkling of a small light. Both of them started walking with fast steps. He felt as if someone was coming behind him, even the rustle of clothes seemed sharp to the ears in the silence. The breath is there. The ears became more alert. The sound of ghungroos, sometimes from far away and sometimes from near, was filling the heart with terror. Both were sweating but hands and legs were trembling. He began to explain to his mind that perhaps there are many crickets in this village, that's why Sultan asked - "You are feeling the same as I am feeling" He could not hide his fear."Yes it looks like someone is there. Don't look back"Holding the hand of his companion Sultan tightly, tearing his throat and reciting Hanuman-Chalisa, he started running with tears in his eyes. He got breathless after running continuously for an hour. Couldn't even see the stone lying in front of him and fell down on his face with a thud that's why it felt like someone put a hand on his shoulder. He screamed loudly, his voice felt as if he was choked in his throat.

"What happened dear, why are you crying?" the house lady asked shrugging his shoulders. His belly was tied, no sound was coming out of his throat. Seeing Rosie Aunty in front of his eyes, he hugged her like a small child hugs his separated mother."Oh! Thank God I survived," he muttered.

*****

CHAPTER ELEVEN

CARETAKER

Hearing a familiar screeching sound outside the door, I became alert that he had come again. My guess turned out to be correct. The doorbell made me get up. He stood at the door knowingly and entered inside as if he is the owner of the house and he has full right to come inside."What's the matter, won't you ask me to sit?""What can I say, you have already sat down" he smiled softly without blinking. Even his smile was giving birth to hatred towards him within me like double meaning signals."Hey! It look like have some relation with you.""I have told you before that you are nothing to me. The woman with whom you had a relationship is no longer in this world, so my relationship with you is over from this point of view as well."

**

I must have been about three years old when my father died. At that age, I did not know how lonely a woman is, when her husband leaves. What she loses, what she suffers, what tragedies she has to go through. I just used to think that my father has passed away, so now who will take me for a walk on his shoulders or who will swing on the swing by sitting on his legs before going to sleep at night? And who will sing? -- Play play by wandering Swing swing in the Ganga Mother Ganga gives us sand We built a wall from sand........Oh! the wall made from sand has fallen"....Saying that father made me fall on the bed, then both of us rolled around laughing. This game would go on till the mother's sleep was not disturbed."Now stop playing, I'm sleepy."

***

"Papa, whose tree is this?""Son, this is a mango tree, we water it daily, we serve it, then after a few years it will give sweet fruits to all of us."So many memories start intruding in the mind in a single moment.

***

It is not known whether it is a mango tree now or not, the one who watered it had gone far away. I didn't know that time that my wall is actually made of sand and will really fall down and how can a child see himself buried under a pile of sand and lose his existence due to the fall of his wall and he can't do anything. This is what I feel even today. I saw mother's travelling from home to office and from office to home. I understood much later when I was sent away from home to study in a boarding school and why I was sent!

When I had to come home on holidays, Keshav Kaka, an elderly acquaintance whom I had been seeing since childhood, was an important part of this house, he would take me home and drop me off at the hostel. When I came home for the first time after my father's departure, the house seemed a bit changed. The color of the house, the decorations, everything seemed new. The sadness on mother's face had also gone away. On seeing me, she started crying out of happiness and immediately hugged me. The stranger entered the house without ringing the bell and looked at the mother with a smile and sat on the sofa next to the mother."Manu! He is Narendra uncle. Say namaste to him."Greeting that person, I was surprised to see him because he was sitting next to my mother on the sofa, talking to her very intimately, which my childhood mind did not like at all. Before this I had neither seen him nor heard his name from father or mother. Mother had also never told about him. Many questions were arising in my mind which were troubling me. My curiosity was probably understood by the mother, so she only told me that "He is my friend and sometimes he comes to meet me at home."

I was no longer a child, I had crossed the threshold of adolescence, knowingly or unknowingly there were many secrets of life that I had become aware of. He stayed for some time then he went out and he did not come for the whole day I was at home. My vacation was over but the whirlwind of questions in my mind was not going to calm down."Keshav Kaka! Which uncle he is?""What to tell now, uncle is there......so he is. What will you do after knowing?" Saying this he avoided my question. Even after reaching the hostel, my mind was restless, there were some questions for which I needed answers. I again started looking for an excuse to come home, now I had grown up in my eyes, could come alone anywhere. Several months passed in this tension that what should I do, I suddenly reached home one day on the pretext of ill health.Someone else had taken the place of father on the nameplate of the door of the house in which father's existence was present in the form of a picture, today that illusion was also broken because a living person had taken the place of the picture in this house. My sudden arrival did not make the mother happy as much as she was surprised. Realizing my state of mind, mother broke the silence."Look Manu, I wanted to tell you but could not. I thought that when you become a little wiser, I will be able to sit face to face and explain to you properly that after the departure of the husband. How difficult it becomes for a woman to live, she is like an empty plot which everyone wants to grab and erect their boundary wall. I don't know whether you will accept it or not." Mother became silent after narrating her past incidents in one breath as if she had lightened herself by throwing out the burden of wallgrains of emotions suppressed within her for years. But what about me. Now she was probably waiting for my reaction, I could say something, that's why the same man who was sitting inside the bedroom, listening to us, came out from the living room. Today, for the second time, he and I came face to face and I started handling my abnormal state of mind. At that time it seemed to me that time had made me grow up ahead of time.I didn't find anything in that person that could pull me towards him, don't know what mother saw in him, it was beyond my imagination...Maybe she felt safe by staying with him, but how could I intentionally give the place that my father had in my mind to someone else, my heart completely rejected this idea."Mom, it's your life live it the way you want to live it I can't force you to accept my views and neither can you force me."Saying this I picked up my suitcase and left."Where is going, Manu?" "I can't stay here because I don't want your married life to have some problem because of me. Anyway a hotel room will be enough for me."

The bitterness that was in my mind was being expressed by my words, I don't know whether anyone felt it or not but I wanted them to feel. I deliberately walked away without looking at my mother, as if I was looking for an excuse to hurt my mother to ease the pain of the hurt on my heart. I knew she wanted to say something to me but I ignored her and went out like a defeated warrior fighting with myself and returned to the hostel without telling my mother before the vacation was over.

It was not acceptable for me to enter the territory of my heart unauthorizedly. It was also not in my nature for someone to join my life against my will, that's why there was no crowd of friends around me, there was only one friend and that too was a room partner.This time, after returning from home, my mind was very disturbed, but in spite of all this, the pang of guilt kept reminding me repeatedly that I had not done right by coming here without telling my mother. Shubham, my room partner realized this that something is troubling me so much that I can't even sleep at night. This year was the final year but I did not feel like studying at all."What's the matter Manas? I see that you are very much disturbed since you came home. If you want to tell me, you can."While solving the knot of a question, every page of my life kept opening in front of him, which I had kept suppressed inside me for years."Look, whatever happens in our life, it is not necessary that it is according to our wish. Whatever happens, you may agree with it or not, but according to your priority, you have to accept or reject it, then here the question is with your mother. I can understand that you are not able to accept this truth. You are not a child anymore, you have grown up. It was a small seedling, with the increase of your age, it has also turned into a strong banyan tree, but you will have to find a cure for it, you will have to uproot it." "Thanks Shubham, I think it's okay," saying this I left the room.The more I tried to feel myself closer to my mother, a wretched shadow would come and stand between me and her. However, I did not want that the Lakshman line of hatred had been drawn between me and my mother should remain even. I knew that if this did not happen, the credibility of the blood relationship between mother and son would become a joke. For which my own father, wherever he is, will never forgive me.I would often call my mother and talk to her, ask about her health, but no one mentions about that man. Mother also knew this, so she also did not take his name in front of me.After finishing my final year, I wanted to go abroad on fellowship for higher education.I also got a chance for that. I was very ambitious since childhood. Now I had only one goal to know the people of the outside world and understand their psychology. I was fed up with the current phase of my life I was going through. I had to break free from the cobwebs of despair and hopelessness. I wanted to get out of it and prove myself in a new direction in a new environment. I used to think that I would have to come out of my shell to give new flight to my wings. I had informed my mother on the phone that naturally she was very happy.Six months after I went abroad, nature played such a game with me that I could not understand whether this punishment was given to me or my mother or that other person. Mother had left this world forever. My misfortune did not give me a chance even for the formalities and I was left heartbroken.

After two years I returned to my country with a good job, but from the dark well of sadness and despair, I had come out to fly in a new sky, in that the inner heat of guilt increased, which made me even more angry and started burning day and night. The job of a multinational company had all the luxuries but there was no one to share the happiness with, not even me.

Look at tye cycle of nature, the city from which one day I wanted to run away and lose myself in the crowd of the world. The time had again braught me in the same city and after so many years before that man in front of him and made him stand infront of me.

***

"Whether your job is going well?" "This is none of your business to ask me?"

His words were bothering me. In my view, this person was the reason for the distance between me and my mother. He had distanced me from my mother."It doesn't matter if you come down now on you. My purpose in coming is not to make you sad. I had to fulfill your mother's last wish." Saying this he held a thick envelope in my hand and got up and left.

Unwillingly, I opened the envelope and found some government papers, the key chain of the house which had evicted me from my own house many years ago and a letter..."Dear Manas!Calling you by your name will be enough because you have not given me the right to call you son. I know what you think about me. And even while reading this letter, your heart must be filled with hatred towards me. Never mind, today I forgive you for everything that you have done knowingly or unknowingly in your life, including the trouble you gave to your mother. which she didn't even deserve. Your mother and I used to work in an office and we were just friends and after the death of your father, your mother had only one purpose in her life until her son was able to take care of her, I will be care taker of her. And to save her from those people who were keeping their evil eye on her. I was her care taker till her son became an adult. As a friend, it was my duty to protect her from the prying eyes of people. She used to do a job so that she could make you stand on your feet by teaching you. Doing job was not her hobby, she was sacrificing herself in the sacrificial altar of struggle and nothing else but I don't know why you or time didn't give her a chance to explain to you about herself and me, maybe she was waiting for the right time. The right time did not come and she left before that.My relationship with your mother may have been that of husband and wife to the world, but I never let it separate her from your father's memories. This truth was as if there is a mango tree planted by your father in the backyard of the house and the vine of Madhumalati is wrapped around it. You may go and see that nowadays it is full of flowers. The rest you are intelligent, you must have understood." ~Narendra

*****

CHAPTER TWELVE

ENOUGH! NOW NO MORE

He started panting while running, he didn't even have time to look back. Holding his breath, he kept running and running. His friend Badri was left behind but his screams followed him. Even after coming far away, Badri's sobbing voice pierced his heart with pain and he felt himself bleeding.As soon as he entered the house, he closed the door, even now he was trembling, it seemed that the rapid pulsation of the veins of the body was making the bellows of the breath faster and faster. "What happened to you, why did you get dressed?" Dullo was shocked to see her husband in such condition. "Tell me something, what happened?"Without saying anything, he silently went to the bungali of the house and lay down covered with a quilt. Even in the quilt, the body was trembling as if a cat was jumping and jumping inside the quilt in search of prey."Wait, I'll make some tea."But he didn't say anything, it was the heat that was increasing. Was it shivering due to cold or was his heart and mind engulfed in the fire of the furnace of terror, which he was hiding inside the quilt and was trying hard to calm down."Why didn't you tell me anything, what happened? After finishing what work, you come?" Dullo said while keeping the cup of tea on the ground. Then hearing the voices of the people outside the door, he became more restless and muttered with trembling lips."Don't open, don't open the door. They'll kill me.""Whom do you talk about? Who will kill you?"He calmed down for a while. Dullo started rubbing her forehead."No one is at the door, come on, get up and have the tea. It will reach some rest in your heart." He sat up.

A sip of tea filled the body with a little warmth within him and at this time he was not even alone. After getting the support of his wife's two words of affection, the fear had reduced a bit and he was also feeling some consciousness. He sat for a long time in the quilt with his knees pressed to his stomach. At this time, he was thinking that it is wrong to be afraid without committing a crime, but how to get out of the trouble in which he was trapped at this time. His face had turned snow white as if all the blood in his body had frozen like water."What you have done? Why are you not telling anything?" Dullo became teary-eyed.Without saying anything, he lay down quietly and, exhaling long breaths, started muttering again in his sleep."They must have killed Badri, they will kill me too."Simple Dullo could not understand what he is saying, why is he so scared."Have you come here after quarreling with someone?"After a while he sat up again as if a bad dream had woken him up.Badri's painful screams were ringing in his ears as if a lot of ear-palms had attacked both his ears which were not letting him sleep.The sound of 'Satak-Satak' created mutiny in the mind and the panic in the heart was burning his body."You have high fever, come on, get up and bring medicine from the doctor.""No, I didn't go anywhere. You put a cold water bandage on my head, I will be fine." Dullo sat all night doing cold water bandage, now the day was about to break. He slept peacefully. She lay down to straighten up, but where is the sleep in her eyes? She had sent the piece of her heart away from her by keeping a stone on her chest, but today the same chest was demanding an account of her affection from her.

**

"Why are you hanging your face, Lalla?" "I will not go to school from tomorrow, mother!" Nihal started crying loudly hugging mother's chest."Tell me right, what happened?" "Why don't school children play with me, mother! I have never fought with anyone, then why do children do this to me." "No problem, Lalla! We will put you in another school."At that time, Dullo coaxed him into silence, but after that she did not sit silent until she sent her son away from here to study in the city.

He and his wife Dullo had only one aim in life to give a respectable life to their son who was studying in the city and they did not want the shadow of their family work to fall on their son Nihal, so they had sent him for study at the place of their distant uncle who was living in the city and who used to work as a guard in a company.

****

When his eyes opened in the morning, he was not able to get up as if someone had taken away all the strength of his body, still he got up from the bed. The incident of the previous day was not taking the name of leaving his mind, at the same time Badri came inside the house, pushing the door hard, he jumped with happiness seeing Badri in front of him."Hey brother, you have come! Are you okay?""Yes, I am fine. I came to tell you that the Sarpanch's cow has been found. The cow had gone far away while grazing."On hearing this, a wave of happiness ran in his body. The body which till now was not able to lift the weight of his legs, in a moment that body became very light. The morning which was looking dirty in the fog of fear, was filled with light and now it was starting to feel good.

Seeing the blue marks of injury on Badri's body, Dullo understood why her husband was trembling so much at night."I told you many times to leave this job but you did not listen to me. Someone skinned animals and others beat them. I consider such work as a sin anyway, but it did not enter your mind. I have told you many times to take another job, but you have not listened. It is good that my son is not here.""Just keep quiet too, you are talking again and again" he interrupted his wife."You know that people are not ready to give any work to our caste. You are knowing that outside world is how much merciless and unsweetened. You just make bread, this is your work, leave the rest on me, I know what to do" Having said this, he went out with Badri to take stock of the outside world, but he still felt as if people's eyes were following both of them.

Sarpanch's cow was found but he was worried about his future bread and water. If he does this dirty work to earn bread, then on the other hand, people outside the caste look at him with suspicion and hatred. The housewife has also kept some bickering every day.He is also fed up with this work. The stench of rotten meat in the air of Chamartola seems to have lodged its folds in both his lungs, which will not be able to come out till death.He stayed for a while and the craving for tobacco took him to Kalicharan's kiosk, where both of them took turns smoking tobacco-filled cheroots as if they would be able to get rid of the stench of rotten flesh by inhaling it. He was not satisfied with that either. "Friend Kali! give me a paan masala with fragrance."He pressed half a packet of pan masala to his cheek and handed over the rest to Badri."See what kind of smell it is, you also put it in your mouth, all the dirty smell will go away."

**

The work of lifting the dead animal in the village was also the responsibility of any one class among the Dalits. If one got fifty to sixty rupees for lifting a dead animal, then one could have lived by pulling it, but it is a bad, infamous, bad thing, if someone's animal dies by its own death or if someone's animal is lost, then only those people are blamed who used to dispose of their dead bodies. It was on that day that the Sarpanch's cow went missing that the needle of suspicion fell on Badri and on him. He somehow managed to escape but Badri was surrounded by the Sarpanch's men. It was happened good that in the evening, men of Sarpanch reached there and Badri's life was spared.

He had not got any work for many days. Stuck in the quagmire of the situation, he was not able to understand what to do.Due to the non-repayment of the previous loan, no partner was ready to lend money to him.No money was left to spend at home. The feet themselves moved towards the godown versus the factory, as the smell of rotten meat grew thicker as it approached the factory. The skins hanging on the walls of the godown seemed to be teasing him, the piles of bones surrounded him, the lumps of meat filled with blood everywhere, he started feeling nauseous, he took off his towel and wrapped it around his nose. Bhulla, the owner of the godown, said as soon as he saw him coming."O man! Why did forget the way?" "What should I do? This hunger is very shameless, its fire has made me shameless too. If there is any work, tell me." "Go and get to work skinning in." "No! This will not work for me, tell me another."Bhulla started laughing showing his thirty-two."Don't do your own thing in this business. Whatever work comes your way, it should be done by thumping your chest, otherwise you will be caught on suspicion of stealing and then you will be beaten to death. You both survived that day. If the Sarpanch's cow had not been found that day, you both would have been blamed for killing the cow and both of you would not have survived. You know, right?" "You tell me if you want to bring the animal from somewhere, then send me along with others, but I will not be able to do this." "What should I do? I am not sitting here to do the business of killing animals unnecessarily. Let us pick up only those who die of their own death. Don't eat my head. You run away from here." Having said this, Bhulla went inside. He sat outside holding his head. His own understanding had given the answer what to do, in the meantime Bhulla came out and took him inside holding a knife in his hand."You see, they are also working" said pointing towards others.

His hands were trembling while holding the knife. He had not done this work before, he was in so much trouble. He was watching others work very carefully, he felt as if his body was being peeled. The pain he was going through breaking inside and people were not aware of it. When he thought that there is nothing to eat in the house, so he strengthened his mind and started using the knife. In a short spell of time, something shocked him, as if he woken up from sleeping. Very quickly he escaped from there and anyhow by taking street of his house he reached on the door of his. On the door Dullo was available. She screamed when she saw him..."What is this? You have done dirty work. Get away from me! What kind of smell is coming from you."

The bloodstains on his clothes had put the stamp of a crime which he had not committed. How could he tell Dullo that he had run away from there. He has not done this work and this work was not possible by him. The flood was taking him in the direction where all the embankments break and there is no other option but to drown, he started feeling his life useless. Surrounded by the darkness of helplessness, he was disgusted with himself.Unaware of the eternal truth of life's impermanence, today's heinous act weighed so much in the scales of his conscience that his own life became meaningless and light, and he began to gamble his life like a loser.He started thinking to end his self life, at the same time Dullo, like a ray of light, pulled him out of the darkness and made him sit under the sharp edge of the tap, but even the water could not clean the stains on his body and mind. He entered the bungali and started crying bitterly. Hearing his voice, Dullo came running inside. Seeing his condition, her hate immediately went away, despite the hate that had developed some time ago towards him. She hid the hate in her chest. The mire in which the feet have been sinking for years and which had drowned till the neck, how would he get out of it. Sleep was far away from the eyes of both the husband and wife. The whole night was spent awake waiting for the morning.

Before dawn, Dullo came and stood in front of him after taking a bath and filling a bag with some necessary clothes and things."Get up, no more, further no." He joined Dullo by holding hands like a small child without saying anything. Beyond the horizon to another world where one can get clean air to breathe. The darkness of his mind had dispelled, now he wanted to live. Before dawn they both set out on the footpath leading away from the village.

***

He was wandering in the streets of the past, as the doors of memories kept opening, the speed of tears in his eyes was increasing and he was crying bitterly.

The stage of the convocation ceremony was decorated, the whole hall was packed, in the midst of this commotion, the sound of applause and the sound coming from the stage disturbed his sleep.....''Mr Nihal Kumar Post Graduate Economics Gold Medalist.''He was still sitting on the chair like a statue, on hearing the name of his son, he was shocked and jumped from the chair with happiness. As if he had woken up from a dream, both his cheeks were wet with tears.''Papa, this is for you.'' Nihal put his medal around his father's neck and hugged him.

Today he was missing Dullo very much because today Dullo's dream was fulfilled but he did not know that among the countless stars in the sky, there was one star which shone brighter than others and indicated to join their happiness.

*****

CHAPTER THIRTEEN

PARTY NIGHT

"Why today is salary day, isn't it?" Bindli lovingly asked her husband Raghuram."Yeah, what's new?"Bindli was thinking that if she gets salary, she will settle the old accounts of the tradesman and bring some bargains.It is also a crime to go in front of God without a bright face. This is the tradesman who can get the price of mustard seeds from one pie. It is a very easy task for the long hands of dishonesty to extract a mouthful from the throat of the helpless poor. But Bindli is helpless, what to do, she gets involved in the makeshifting of feeding five persons and listens to the rebuke of the owner of the only shop in the colony and sometimes she abuses with her whole heartedly. But whenever the miserly shopkeeper felt pity for the halal goats, that shop of the shopkeeper would have become an open door to Annapurna Maiya's store, then she would have blessed him a lot. Hunger does not allow anyone to stand up straight with his head raised, but accepts it only after falling on the feet. Harshburnt hunger clings to the body like a torn rag on the skins which you wear it, will be naked and take it off, will be completely naked.

Slender Raghuram works as a cumbersome mason at Kashiram's brick kiln. He has a defect in one leg since birth. Because of one leg being a little short, he walks with a limp. In a 10 by 10 hut, he lives with his wife Bindli, the boy king and his old parents. There is a small courtyard in the backyard of the hut, there is a mud stove in one corner, next to the sack, a tap at the bathing place, which is of the municipality and which had installed in her house along with the people of the colony by paying a lot of money, otherwise everyone had to bring water from the nook corner of the street.

The eleven-year-old Raja used to go to school in the township, but he was more engrossed in sports than studying there. The burden of books to carry was more heavy for his light mind than for his shoulders.

The blurred vision of the old parents is such that it is difficult to identify who has come and who has gone until someone comes near and calls. As soon as a piece of dry bread is found, they become patient and both of them never fail to thank the God that he had given so much. But there would have been a day when they too would not have had any luck, thinking that they would have been hit by their false luck, they would have silently crouched inside their dolls with their stomach pressed in their knees, only these words would have come out of their mouth that now the God has lifted them up.

Bindli's life was like grains grinding in the dust of the house, the more it grinds, the more it loses its existence and becomes like dust. Grinding between life and its fate was her destiny and when the person bound by destiny reaches the limit of his/her helplessness. He/she forgets himself/herself in the same way as a grain of grain stuck between the millstones forgets its former existence while being crushed.

Bindli was sitting thinking that how much money Raja's father would bring in her hand today. Last month, the drunkard had reduced his attendance for work, "this time don't deduct daily wages, I beg you God with folded hands" with folded hands towards the sky, Bindli again became engrossed in thoughts. Last month, he was lying at home for ten days after drinking raw liquor, rolling on the floor in the shed, howling and vomiting all night long....."The whole kurta was full of rot, with such difficulty I had removed it from his body by tying a palla on my nose. Drunker, lying unconscious, was neither conscious of his body nor of his clothes. I dragged him to a corner and washed the whole courtyard, then pulling a bucket on myself, what kind of hell did I get rid of by putting it above. With how much effort I took him to the bed, this is the life of a woman and my life was devastated. Even today, if I remember that incidence, I should stop shivering.'" He was not able to go to work for so many days, then even at that time Bindli had to get arranged medicine with her hidden earnings. It is good that the chieftain of the head of the settlement sometimes gives the work of grinding pulses without spices, and then earns a lot of money, but she has neither given the inkling of this to her man, nor does her old mother-in-law and old father-in-law. She keeps in her entanglement. It is not known when some calamity will break like it broke last month Raghu's medicine and liquor on which all the money had spent.

In the meantime, Raja came from the school and the bag like a donkey swinging on his shoulder put on the ground and came.

Bindli had gone to the shop of the tradesman today with a great hope that if he shows some kindness, arrangements for food and water will be made, but he was ready to pounce."You will get the deal only after clearing the previous account, it is your heart that is dealing with that lame drunkard. By the way, let me tell you about my heart, I should not see your in sorrow and understand it! If you don't do something, then I will talk to him. I will put his wisdom in place." At first Bindli kept on listening and then she started saying witu crying, "Hey, why did I come to make a deal with you, you started making a deal with me. Have you understood that there should be no respect for the poor and who are you to say even a word to my man. We have not eaten anything in free and money had been given to you. Today the time is bad, so your tongue has also started fluttering, Lala! You go to the stove and your shop goes to hell."

Bindli understood that this scoundrel's vision is not clear, she returned home on the back foot, it was still on the way that it came to mind that she should stay with the chieftain, maybe if she gets some work, then money will come in her hand."Ram Ram, Mukhiayin!""After a long time, I have seen your face, something special has happened.""I thought, I would get some work here" Bindli sat down on the ground near her chair, looking at the colorful flowers in the beds in front of her, she felt happy and started thinking how lucky the chieftain is to have such a big room to take a bath and a separate cell for sleeping, a separate place of the stove. At the same time a girl appeared in front of her who was sprinkling water in the courtyard and watering the plants. At the same time chieftain scolded her, "stop, will you keep pouring water? Go and put pulses on the stove, it is time for my husband to come." And then she turned to Bindli and said, "Look, rani, now I have no work for you. This girl has been sent from my village by my brother. She is poor orphan, no father, no brother, she stay with me, do all the housework too. Now you go this time. If there is any work for you, I will send you a message. The day is hidden, your husband must also be coming."

Bindli returned with a face like her own. The face was lowered, the legs were not rising, as if someone had tied a stone to the leg, it became heavy to hold the house. There was one last hope, that too was over.

****

"Why Raghu? Do you walk with me? Today is the day of celebration."Raghuram understood for which celebration Puran was talking about. All he wanted to hear was 'celebration day', his whole body shuddered, the body became so light as if it was not walking but was flying in the air. At the same time suddenly Bindli's face appeared in front of his eyes and he fell on the ground with a thump."No no, I have to go home friend, there is no ration water in the house, wife must be waiting for me."

"Hey go away, which leg of yours am I holding. Let's have a little sightseeing of wineshop, there you will get intoxicated by the smell of the air. Come on, don't know if a peg will get excited just by seeing others drinking?"Puran forcefully held Raghu's hand and turned towards Chamrapatta lane.'Puran is saying rightly, what is the harm in passing through there, I am not a child, that someone will forcefully pour it into my throat. I wonder what the hell was going through last month. Because of me the poor wife was also in trouble.....'

"Hey come come, Elders."Kalu wrestler's hank started groping for a spark from the extinguished fire."Hey, I carry the burden for the whole month, if I break my body, then I have the right to recover a little bit. What about bread and water, wife will take care of it. She is a very nice woman of the colony and is not like the clothes that sometimes she can even slap. The one above is very kind, who is tied wife with me like a cow and on top of that, the old parents are also such that whose tongue always sticks to the palate. The satisfaction is so much that even the burning sensation of hunger cools down by going to their wash. Even if spend ten to twenty rupees today, which mountain will break." Raghu's mind got busy in cooking imaginary casserole."Why Puran? What can you say?" asked Raghu, downing his glass full."Oh, about what? I didn't hear." Puran said taking a long sip.Raghu was comforting himself by talking to himself."Will you have one more?" said Puran, probing Raghu.Raghu pushed forward the glass."Come on, if you say so, I will take it, you are my true friend, so I can't break your heart, can I?" "Friend Puran, it is too late, I have to go home too, I will have to walk all night, I have no life in my feet."

Due to the intoxication of alcohol, his senses started getting lost and Raghu even forgot that his hut was only a hundred meters away from here."Let's get up! I have to close the wineshop, do you intend to stay for the whole night? Your mother or wife is not sitting here who will feed you bread and get out of here."The wrestler-like owner of the wineshop held both of them tightly and showed them the way out."Hey friend Puran, today you must have added tadka to the lentils. Come on, you too, come with me. You are my true friend, don't you! You care for me so much. If there is a feast for you today, what will you remember? In the happiness of getting salary she must not have made bread even after counting, we will eat it to our heart."

When Raghu was about to stumble and fall in the imaginary casserole, Puran took care of him with both hands while fulfilling his friendship-religion."Today is the night of celebration, your feast is made.""Yes friend, if you are telling the truth then you must be telling the truth, if I go then it is okay, but your wife will not like it." "Oh no, she is a simple cow, like the one who honks. Yours must have a habit of kicking, but me isn't."They kept humming each other's shoulders with great satisfaction."We will not break this friendship...." then suddenly Raja was found on the way who had left the house to find his father."Bapu! where are you going, you have come home, here you are, your door is right in front of you." "Yes yes come on."Staggering Raghu pushed the door open as if he had won a war. Bindli's body felt such a current in his unsuccessful attempt to embrace Bindli that he fell far away. The dirty smell of wine spreaded in the hut and It did not take even a moment for the woman whom he used to behave arbitrarily considering as a cow, has become Chandi. Bindli rushed at him like a lioness with a broom."Mouth-jhausa! You touch me? You Drunkyard. Fire will come in your mouth. The blind of the eye is not mine, not of this child, but did not even think of the dry bowels of old man and woman. For twenty-four hours, not a single grain has gone into the mouth. Less luck now. You have come in the middle of the night, that too drunk." Bindli's anger was not going to calm down. She started hitting Raghu with the broom more and more forcefully as if she was casting off a ghost."Today I will remove all your intoxication that you will forget alcohol for the rest of your life. What did you think that if I do not speak, then I do not know. You have forgotten that if a cow gives milk, but when you oppress it, you will be kicked as well."

Seeing the rain of the broom on Raghu, Puran thought it will be right to move away from there."Where are you running Drunkyard. You had found my husband in vain to make friend" after beating, Bindli, who became a lioness, threw Raghu on the ground.

Bindli did not know when Puran, who was standing in the corner seeing Raghu being beaten up, slipped away from there, otherwise the flames of anger were so strong that it was impossible to escape the root of all the trouble today. When she got tired of beating the man, she sat down to meditate."How can I pull the cart after dying. I can neither see my body nor my mind, nor can I see day or night. Why wouldn't he has fed botulism all four of us?" Bindli's anger was not over yet. Bindli was crying out as if her long-held desires, which she had suppressed till today, were bursting like havoc today. Raja was standing like a statue in the corner, he understood that even today he will have to sleep on an empty stomach and he went and entered his bed.

When midnight passed and the fire cooled down a bit, she felt conscious and she went to see husband whether he was alive or dead. She went and sat near him, touched and looked, 'Yes, he was breathing, her mind was satisfied. Probably he sleeping in a deep sleep. I am work-fool, why I pill fell on him."

A woman bound by the promise of seven rounds can never get out of the fear that without a man her life is like a loose cow that everyone is eager to tie her with their peg. Bindli looked lovingly at Raghu sleeping on the open floor. Kept caressing her body for a long time, then covering the sheet kept staring at her for a long time. Till a while ago, no one came to know when the woman, whose husband used to drink, came next to her husband and put her hand on his shoulder and fell asleep.

*****

CHAPTER FOURTEEN

THAT STRANGER

Even today the door of the adjacent flat was closed, as it usually remains closed, there is no sign of any sound from inside and no external movement, yes sometimes the sound of a woman's cry definitely comes, that too as if someone is reciting a funeral. This mystery was slowly deepening and was also creating curiosity. Four flats on one floor were also lying closed, as if someone had bought them and put them up to save their income tax. The flat in front of me used to cry sometimes, who had taken it, but whoever had taken it, it was not known who the people were, but today ten to twelve pairs of slippers were testifying outside the same house. That the house is not empty, people live in it too, let there be some brightness in the neighborhood, otherwise there is ghostly silence, well, I shook my mind and got busy with my work. Sunday is a relaxing day for those going to work. Life goes on in its routine and it gets used to it too.

Four months ago suddenly one day I came across a woman in the stairs, slim body can't be called a girl, she can't be of age neither of a young woman nor of an adult, but the attraction was amazing, a salty water was floating in her eyes.

**

"Are you new?" I asked her."Yes I have come from outside."I wasn't expecting such a short answer, thought she would get some introduction and she would also like to know about her neighbor i.e. me."Hey wait wait! Who's in the house?" Making a gesture of two with her hand, she went inside as if a ghost was following her. There was something in her personality that made me think that her behaviour was not normal, either she was stealing glances from people or she was banned from meeting anyone. Having heard and heard some things, it was definitely read in the ears that the husband is a very drunkard. He beats her and abuses are also given by him saying that she is infertile.

Two months passed in the busyness of my job like birds fly away without even realizing it. For a few days now, the fragrance of frankincense incense, sometimes the smoke of fragrant incense sticks would have spread in the whole staircase, then it would have seemed that someone is conducting a ritual of worship in front. This process continued for many days. One such day was a Sunday and I was in a quandary as to what kind of worship takes place in the neighborhood for which closing the door is as necessary as the possibility of disturbance in the so-called worship due to the sight of some ill-fated person. I don't know why I was in an uproar, Sunday may be a day of rest for my mind, getting rid of the daily boring routine, the mind wants to do some new pastime. What does this woman look like to me, why does my attention go towards that stranger neighbour again and again. Generally anyway, the more thoughts we want to avoid, the more they surround us, perhaps it is also that an empty mind is the house of the devil, in the meanwhile the doorbell rang to free me from this devil. I woke up and felt for a moment as if the bell of a temple had rang and after listening to which the consciousness had awakened and returned and my mind would get some peace."Namaste madam ji" "Ramwati! How long have you come here? Are you watching what time is it?" "Yes ma'am, it is late, the aunty of number 10 had stopped me." "She stopped and you stopped? Why? Today is a holiday, so doesn't it mean that you will come according to your own convenience?" "Hey madam, the one who has come to your front house, he is a man of great tantra-mantras, there is a lot of fragrance of frankincense incense sticks, these days there is a lot of aroma. The aunty of 10 number was saying that he keeps his wife in the curtain and because of this fear he is doing worship." The tape recorder of Ramrati's bubbling kept on playing and I started thinking that the mysterious illusion that had entangled me since morning and removed the oil from my mind, let the bell ringer pull me out of this dark cave, but it did not happen, even while working, her legend keep on going.Whispers started happening in the society, people weighed on the criteria of their mentality and did not consider themselves less than a judicial officer. Some people are fond of peeping into other's house, but they forget the windows of their own house.

My life was going on normally. It was my destiny to pull myself together after Abhay left my life and two years have passed since this incident. After Abhay's betrayal I was moving like the needle of the clock, it kept moving at a fixed speed and this was the truth of my life, but gradually the loneliness of my life became the truth of my soul and started immersing me in depression, which I rejected in time and immersed myself in the job. My job became the support of my drowning boat to reach some shore, today it has become the companion of my happiness and sorrow, and sometimes on the day when it was a holiday, then time used to bite me. Now again and again the only thought is coming that I should change the house where there are neighbours and there is tinkling noise of children.

One day while returning from office, I suddenly encountered that stranger neighbour. Last time when she bumped into me on the stairs, she ran away like lightning in the blink of an eye as if lightning would burn her not me, but today nothing like this happened. She greeted me with folded hands which I liked very much as I was not expecting it at all."How are you?""I'm fine."Asking a stranger 'how you are', is nothing more than a formality. Still, I took the matter further and asked."You didn't tell your name that day. Tell me what's your name?" "My name is Vinodini, everyone in the house used to call me Bitto.""Everyone used to call! What does it mean?"A faint smile on her face had expressed her pain."Yes, now there is no one, who will call me Bitto."

Last time, the eyes in which the sea was rolling with the hilarious waves of saltiness, the same eyes were like a dry river in which the sandy desert was merged. There was a difference between the sky and the underworld, let alone the underworld, in today's Vinodini, who was smelling like a spring of that day's delighted monsoon. The eyes which attracted me that day, today those same eyes surprised me.I sat down in the park and she also followed me as if she wanted to say something to me. Pain buried in the heart find a way out, it does not see the opportunity nor does it see the place. The rapid flow of the river ignores the dam and sometimes breaks all the bonds and escapes."Don't you want to go home today?""No, today my husband has gone out.""Do you work, sister?" She asked me a question. The way I was curious to know about my neighbour, it must also be very informal in the second meeting itself. Addressing me as sister was giving an introduction to her intimate feeling. Accepting her intimacy, I also sat down and asked in a natural way."Who do you have at home?""No one, but me and my husband.""That means your parents or siblings will also be there?"

It was natural to have sympathy in the heart for the sequence of events running on the axis of her life circle, about which she started telling me."I was very loved of my parents, but the day my own mother left this world, my fate changed. Father brought another woman in the house. I was not liked by my step mother, she cursed me all day long, all the household work was expected from me by her.At night, when father would return home, she would make him intoxicated with her own hands and I could not say anything to my father. The father of whom I was once daughter Bitto, had stopped talking to me and looked at me far away. What a spell that cruel woman had cast on my father." She again said, "My stepmother made me drop my studies and gave my hand to this man to pay off her debt and I was told that his first wife had died two months ago."

While narrating her true-story, she suddenly stopped, as if she wanted to pacify the whirlwind that arose in the heart, but once the whirlwind arises, then it goes on increasing without looking ahead and behind, wasting so much as a blindly."What does your man do?" "He drives a taxi.""Do you both pass on that earning?" "I have heard that there is some farming in the village and..." ".... and what else?"She remained silent for some time and said wiping her eyes."I came to know later that my husband's first wife is not dead, she is childless and lives in the village. It is my bad luck that my father's second wife has sold me to him for money." "Are you happy?" "What about my happiness!""There also I used to clean utensils, I used to worl all day, here I do the same and in temptation I break my body too." "Why don't you complain to the police?" "How can I do that, sister! This must have been written in my part, if this had not happened, would it have been my fault?" "This is the problem of women like you, keep on bearing the oppression of the man and blame the fate, that's why the courage of the man increases. If oppression is a crime, then it is equally wrong to tolerate oppression." "No sister, once the respect of a woman is exposed, it becomes like an open shop, I don't want to sell myself anymore." Her words undoubtedly hurt me to the core.

I got up leaving her words incomplete, my head started buzzing. I wanted to shake her true-story out of my mind after coming home, but the more I wanted to leave, the more insistently the thought kept gripping me. In a male dominated society a woman's dignity may be negligible, but where a woman, being an enemy of a woman, pushes herself into such a well where she becomes breathless even after being alive, it is better that nature should make her a dog or a cat than such a cursed female body.

***

Since few days I was feeling that whenever I open the door, two eyes are peeping at me through the wrinkles, trying to say something, I cannot say for sure, maybe it is my illusion.One day I was going out to collect my luggage and suddenly it seemed that someone was calling from the small crackling in the front door. I thought she must be in some trouble but it was not."Yes, do you want to say something?" in my imagination kajal's curls were found on her face, there must have been frozen tears on her face, as

I had heard, the same face was telling something else today, she was shy like a young woman, she just whispered."Good news." In fact, the reddening of her face was also telling the good news.It seemed that the tide of her happiness was getting restless to break the dam and come out, perhaps her time to seize happiness was over. Frustrated husband himself gets frustrated and celebrates his pseudo masculinity by tying the woman in the same chain. Nature had cleaned it very politely today and the auspiciousness of being a complete woman was fixed on her forehead. She was feeling freedom by spreading like a fragrance and wanted to tell everyone that -- 'Look, I am not barren, I am also a complete woman, my husband also loves me.'

She went away after saying good news, but today she had left the door open which was always closed, as if that woman who was bound by the bondage of frustrations had not only got recognition, she had also got the freedom to live with self-respect. By making her my companion, that woman was no longer a stranger to me, but had made a place in some corner of my heart.The red rose of the pot kept outside in the stairs was also a witness, despite being surrounded by thorns, it was giving the message of new life, trying to smile with pride.

*****

CHAPTER FIFTEEN

CRACKLING RELATIONSHIPS

"What's the matter, now you often come home late?" "What should I do? I had a meeting with the boss." "Is there a meeting everyday or is there some work as well at your workplace?" Akash's voice was harsh."Look, if you want to get a job from me, you will have to bear all this. The work is too much, what can I do?" Even Roma could not remain silent."Look Roma, all this will not work everyday, I know who only washes hands in which Ganges and in which bathes. Change your attitude or measure your path."

Whatever happened today, Roma was not expecting it after returning from office. She thaught, Akash who once had so much faith in me that he didn't mind even going on tour with the boss and instead used to say that "It happens in private job that if the company is giving you a package of lakhs, then the oil is also extracted completely."

Such a gross insult under the guise of disbelief. Termites had started appearing in the wall of the relationship, Roma had started to feel some of it for some time. Because Akash was no longer same Akash, the warmth of the relations had started getting cold dampness. Akash, hiding in any corner of the house, was always eager to embrace her in his open arms, and even without wanting to, he had to say, 'Hey go away, someone will see'.

Roma was shocked, but all this would change so soon, Roma did not expect it at all, which happened today. Just like Akash knew that by mercilessly pulling a taunt of the relationship, its web would automatically weaken and break and perhaps he wanted it to break, that's why he is doing this deliberately 'Is he bored with me or somewhere else. ....Roma jerks her brains out 'no no it can't be.'

Akash's mother Sushila Devi was sitting in her room listening to all this and could not believe how her son could stoop to this extent. The only thought that kept haunting her mind was that of Roma for whom Akash had offended and having lifted this house to the seventh sky, had stopped talking to everyone for months, suddenly one day in that house, he went against his Babuji (i.e. father) and made Roma stand in the house in the afternoon.

***

"Roma! Take blessings of Maa-Babuji (mother & father)."The vermilion of demand was itself gossiping about his work.Mother's love is like a stream of oil, wherever it slopes, it will flow.Blessings came out of mother's mouth even though she did not want to be lucky, but Akash's father,Prashantbabu's virility turned red and sat down in a corner cowering in the lurch to handle the remaining days of his life which had come at the mercy of time and old age. The teacher, who taught the world about discipline and principles, had kept silent under the guise of the flow contrary to his own ideology. The dialogue between son and father gradually became non-existent."Babuji is more concerned about his reputation in the society than our happiness, only these neighbors and relatives will sail his boat" "Why are you saying like this son, never say such a bitter thing in front of him, I swear to you." Sushila Devi pleaded with Akash in persuasive words.She said, "What you are today because of his sacrifice and hard work." "Yes, you will take his side only, the person who roams around in the outside world with the medal of progressive thoughts hanging around his neck, who prides himself on showing the direction to the society, the same person inside the four walls of the house should be so well fed up with his own son's marriage in other religions. How can he be against marriage. Well, let it go, mother!" Saying this, Akash went out.

Prashantbabu, who did not get tired of comforting the doors and windows of the house with the cultured voice within the four walls, and the holy waves of Vedic self-respecting shlokas echoed was coming from, now he would sit quietly in his room for hours. In the morning, he used to leave for his school at the appointed time and after returning from school, he sit directly to his study room. He used to immerse himself in the books in which he got the treasure of pearls of knowledge from his childhood till today. As if it was getting out of his hands now. Perhaps, by revisiting them again and again like a dutiful saint, he wants to prove himself fearless from the beatings given by time, establishing his truth and living his familiar self-satisfaction, but this series also slowly started breaking down and the light in the study room often went off.

Sushila Devi used to go and try to convince him by referring to the circumstances."Look, ours time is no longer, the son is young, if he marries on his own wish, then what happened, time is changing. Let him live in his own happiness. Look at the daughter-in-law once, test her, then rightly your perception will change.""During all my life, I followed my principles and those who were my strength, due to which I always lived with my head held high, today the same head has bowed down. People used to give example of commitment to my principles; you will not understand Akash's mother."

Akash and Roma used to work in the same office. Time was moving at its own pace. Prashantbabu also slowly started opening up to his daughter-in-law or it can be said that Roma had won the hearts of both mother-in-law and father-in-law with her good manners-born behavior. A child without parents had found the shadow of parents. An educated girl, the daughter of a well-educated family knew her duties very well."Akash! come early from office today. You have to take Babuji to a Doctor for his check up. I think he is not feeling well. Though he hasn't said anything to anyone, not even your mother.""Why don't you take a leave?" Akash interrupted Roma and said:"Look Roma, today I have a lot of work in the office, I will not be able to come soon.""Ok, I see." Roma didn't expect this answer from Akash at all. She had been leaving behind Akash's irresponsible actions after getting the reward of Babuji's service often in the form of blessings. Roma didn't even know when it became an act of coercion.The change in Akash's nature was not hidden from his mother, but she used to console herself thinking, after listening to frequent quarrels between husband and wife, that this happens between every husband and wife. The closer the utensil collides, the louder it will sound, but still in a corner of the mind, as if something untoward. The knock was unsettling again and again. She reassured herself... 'No it can't happen, I have full faith in my blood.'

***

Roma came home after taking half day leave from her office to take Babuji to the doctor. Today, Sushila Devi was proud of her daughter-in-law that her son did not make a wrong choice by liking Roma. Prashantbabu also thaught that he was sitting unnecessarily with angry. He asked to Sushila Devi,"Akash's mother! At least make tea for daughter-in-law, today she had to come early because of me, ask whether she has eaten food or not?" "Hey Babuji! Why are you saying like this, it is my duty, you are my Babuji." At the same time, Prashantbabu had a cough attack again today after many days and the cough was not taking the name of stopping. Prashantbabu's body was getting weaker since a few days. Initially no one noticed but when the rule of going for daily morning walk started breaking, then it is noticed. His going to school was also decreasing day-by-day. Sushila Devi felt, in her mind, something unusual, why would a person who has been disciplined throughout his life derail his daily routine."Listen, I do not feel well about your health, I have been watching for a few days. If I ask you, you do not tell what is the matter? It is necessary to see a doctor."Dr. Bansal was a family doctor only to show himRoma had come early from office.

According to the doctor, Prashantbabu was affected by cold and his blood pressure was also high."There is nothing to worry. I have given medicine, blood pressure is high, for this, now you have to take medicine regularly"

**

Today, Sushila Devi felt restless due to the crack in the wall of relationship between son and daughter-in-law. The foundation of the house which she and her husband had laid on the bricks of the heritage of principles and human relations, the beginning of shaking, perhaps it had happened a few years ago, which her loving heart was hesitating to accept. And today Sushila Devi was sitting thinking that which termite licked her iron-livered husband and the family could not even know, in front of her.

His picture hanging on the wall often raised these questions for her, the answer of which was found by Sushila Devi today but now it was too late. Now yesterday could not be returned even if we wanted to, but preparations can be made to deal with the coming storm.

Seeing the changing attitude of Akash, Roma could not live for a day."What's the matter, Akash! Why do you keep pulling me so much these days, if there is any problem then tell me.""No, nothing like that" Akash walked out saying as if he had nothing left to say. When the estrangement between husband and wife or the distance between them starts increasing, then the child / children of both of them act as a bridge, which is also natural, but this was not there in Roma's life either. Five years have passed since the marriage, when did five years of life pass in understanding and fulfilling the responsibilities of the job, the disaster of the house, Roma could not know. Today, when the sound of husband's neglect and unexpected desolation started knocking in life, she realized that she had lost more than what she had gained in life. She had heard about extramarital affairs, but adding this to Akash's indifference towards her, she did not want to get trapped in the frustration of inferiority by trivializing her and Akash's relationship. She took the responsibility of her marital relationship very seriously. She wanted to perform, but clapping with one hand is as difficult and impossible as moving forward without taking another step.

Mother Sushila Devi had also started realizing that since many days something inappropriate is happening in the life of son and daughter-in-law that the noises coming from her bed room used to disturb her, but today Akash told Roma that "change your attitude or else measure own way." Sushila Devi was looking at her husband's photo for a while. The dam that was stopped for a long time burst into tears today. Today she was feeling all alone and helpless.The walls of the house had started crumbling from the very day when Prashantbabu breathed his last.

"How can someone show the way out to his wife, okay, if the family line has not progressed in these years, then what happened is the responsibility of both husband and wife. The woman who has been surrendering every moment of her life, every turn of her body every night, her body like the folds of the bed to her husband, the same husband showed her the way out and shattered the glass house like a fish" thinking this her heart was unable to accept this difficult truth that she had been left to suffer. Sleep was far away from Sushila Devi's eyes, she spent the whole night wandering outside the window in the forest of silence.

Akash return from jogging in the morning as usual. When he returned, he was thinking that Roma must be sitting with a cup of tea. This is the quality of time that it does not change its course by asking.

Seeing a big suitcase kept outside in the verandah, Akash muttered, 'Now who is this in the morning?He saw Roma sitting next to the wall near the window of the verandah as if she was staring at him somewhere in the void, today she didn't even have a cup of tea in her hand."Come on Roma" Sushila Devi said pointing towards the suitcase. Akash looked back as soon as he heard his mother's voice."Hey mom! You too? But where?" "Yes me too, but don't ask where? You have lost this right. Till now, I have been sitting like a coward watching a lot of injustice happen. Enough is enough! Now no more, Akash! I know you have gone astray. I am your mother, I know everything. You are now not a child. Akash! You can live by covering the mystery of the life, but not me. Transparency in relationships has always been the capital of my life."

Akash said, "It's good, it's okay." The expression of feelings was forcing the mother to speak a lot but somehow she restrained herself."Not you, someone will have to atone," Sushila Devi said wiping her eyes."Come on daughter, Roma!" Roma went out to breathe in the open air holding the suitcase in one hand and mother's hand in the other.

*****

CHAPTER SIXTEEN

PANDAN

Alok Rai Srivastava is working on the post of Junior Engineer in Municipality and is more simple and honest than necessary. The smell of the officer could not even touch him, in a job in which people put their feet down from their long car only after taking the offer, in the same profession, an honest man like Alokrai does not consider his old gossip to be less than a flying angel. Outside the house of his colleagues, apart from the gleaming flash, two or more vehicles are parked with great pride, but Alok Babu does not have any qualms about this, he believes that, "Dry dry eat sweet sleep"

It hasn't even been six months since he shifted from Sitapur district to Hardoi. It is his daily job routine to go to the field to supervise the site work which he used to do in his old Humsafar motorcycle and this happy-go-lucky ride never gave him a chance to complain. Today, the work assigned to him by his boss is to go outside Hardoi town to survey the construction of Ganga Expressway in Bilgram tehsil. Which Alok Babu gladly accepted, because the land of Bilgram whose blessings and the threads of vows sought in many temples made him a capable person, on that land his family once used to live, the same relationship today he has full attraction. Was pulling along.

Alok Babu reaches home from office and calls his wife from the door itself..."Kusum! where are you? Just do one thing, pack my bag quickly, I have to go out of office for two days." "Where will you go? Will you tell something?" "Yes, I have to go to Bilgram.""Come on, it's good, you had a great desire to see your native land, isn't Bilgram far away?" "No, it will be twenty-seven to twenty-eight kilometers like this, but see, Kusum! how funny it is that I was so busy with my job that I didn't even get to leave. Now I have got a chance. And yes, see that you must keep some food items." Like her husband, Kusum Lata is a simple, religious-minded housewife, who always says yes to her husband's yes, and the meaning of her husband's religion is only in walking half a step behind her husband's footsteps.

"Take your bag is ready, listen, eat your medicine on time" Kusum said with great insistence that only then the sound of car horn was heard from outside the house.

"Sahab, the vehicle has arrived, let's go," Lallan, the driver of the departmental vehicle, shouted loudly. Alokrai went out waving his wife goodbye. Driver Lallan wanted to open the car door but Alok Babu did not like it and he went ahead smilingly opened the door himself and sat in the car.

Alok Babu's old childhood memories were running like a movie in the binoculars of his brain at double the speed with which the car was moving at this time."Why brother Lallan! you must be coming this way.""Yes Sahab, it is our daily work."Twenty-five years ago, this kutcha road had taken his family far away from here, and the same kutcha road that had settled in his mind for years was unrecognizable today, but even after twenty-five years, the soil in which he grew up playing still felt that place. The sweet smell of the same soil in the air was the same; it was filling his heart and mind with excitement by awakening the feeling of belonging."Lallan! Bilgram has changed a lot, now even a tonga does not ply, perhaps not a single one is visible" "No sahab, paved roads have not been made! Now tempo vehicles run at a fast pace. See, that is Peepla Chauraha, it is a very beautiful place here."Like a guide while driving, Lallan was telling about every place where he felt progress had been made.

"You're right, everything seems to have changed"Alok Babu was going on matching his childhood memories and was happy with the progress here, but inside he was feeling empty and strange as if something dear was being left out of his hands. The car was now crossing Sadar Bazar via Ganj Road when seeing the Mansanath temple in front, Lallan slowed down the car and went ahead with folded hands in front of the temple and in a short while went in front of the tehsil and parked the car."Come sahab, Tehsil came and arrangement has been made here for your stay."

Alok Babu got down from the car. When the peon who opened the lock of the room next to the tehsil bowed down and saluted, he could not stop laughing but definitely answered by raising his hand.The air of Bilgram's earth and the smell of the soil here were like a valuable heritage for Alok Babu. But after coming here it seemed that there is nothing left that he can call his own, even if something is left, it is also half incomplete. The raw dusty roads looked like slippery snakes of bitumen. The pleasant little mud houses and thatched roofs giving cool shade outside, under which the elders of the street used to share their joys and sorrows, had today been transformed into houses with concrete gates made of brick and mortar.

"Sahab! didn't you feel happy after seeing our Bilgram?" "Oh no no, it's not like this, there should be progress." but just by saying 'Hamara Bilgram' by Lallan, something broke like a child's favorite toy someone saying that it is mine. Alok Babu himself smiled at this childish thinking of his."Lallan! how far is muhalla Sulhara from here?" "It is not far sahab! there is a walking path, if there is any problem, shall I go with you?" "Oh no I'll go"

Alok Babu left on foot. Old memories started stirring in his mind again. Every year when he used to come back home after spending summer vacations at Nana's place, the experience of sitting in ace to go home from the bus stand used to be very exciting. Sitting on a seat like a high scaffolding carousel, he was feeling the sensation of eating hallar-hallar hiccups and being bathed in the dust of the unpaved road even though there was no dust today. On the way to home, there used to be a competition among all the brothers to pluck mangoes from the mango tree and jamun from jamun trees. Today Alok Babu was laughing thinking how sweet those raw mangoes were. Today there were black flat roads in front and small kiosks of tea and paan tobacco on the side of the road. Orchards laden with fruits had become the gift of progress. Then the school building appeared in front. The school building was in its place, but its color lacquer was telling that now the children must be studying sitting on the bench and table and not on the slap, the school must have also progressed.The way from school to home felt as if one had accidentally entered the street of a strange place. He went a little further towards his locality where small eatables and paan beedi cigarette shops had replaced the lush green mango trees on the banks of Matiyali Dhali. Seeing the hoarding advertising Panmasala in front of him, his mouth became tight. Each brick of the dream house was falling down and someone was trying his best to stop it from falling with all the strength of both his arms. On reaching there, Alok Babu looked around.Most of the houses had turned into mud's duh. Some street children were probably hiding and playing cards in a dilapidated house.

Alok Babu's mind was filled with strange disgust. He had to strain his mind to recognize his house, but seeing the presence of the neem tree, he got some relief. The earthen platform outside the house and the painted thatch over it had been taken over by a concrete platform. The neem tree standing next to it at the turn of the lane leading to Rasoolan Chachi was the only sign that was left of Alok Babu's residence. Later it was found that his house had been bought by some Majeed Lohar.

Kallan Miyan appeared in front of him as soon as he saw him, he also remembered playing Gulli Danda with all the street children. The color of henna in the hair was teasing the white hair of Kallan, the body was slightly full but there was no significant change in the facial features. He asked, "Hey Kallan! how are you?"

Instead of giving an answer, Kallan shot the opposite question, "Srivastava! how are you here?" "I had come for some official work."

Without answering, he went ahead with an indifferent expression on his face as if he no longer remembered how we both grew up playing together, jumping and jumping in the tubewell water. Remembering is a far away thing, he was not even interested in any kind of worldliness, as if someone has forgotten everything by erasing the old text written on the slate and writing a new text.

A lot has changed in the last twenty five years, so many walls have been pulled down, so many relationships have become orphans. Alok Babu's mind was now getting extinguished. Still, he could not give up the desire to meet Rasoolan Chachi, who pampered him in his childhood.

Rasoolan Chachi's house was in a dilapidated condition. Plaster flakes were coming off the walls of the house. Termites had carved vines in the Lakhori bricks. The wooden door was also battered by time. Half of it was hanging in the air with the help of a nail, but thankfully the chain was left.

Alok Babu's inner child couldn't contain himself and he started banging loudly."Who is the nameless came this time?" A woman's hoarse voice came from inside. The door was open and without permission he entered the house like earlier in his childhood he used to visit his aunt ten times a day sometimes through the roof and sometimes through this door fearlessly."Who is it? Why don't you speak?"

Alok Babu fearlessly went and stood in front of the old woman who was lying on a very old bed from the time of Baba-adam. Alok Babu remembered that this is the same bed which was once the center of attraction for all of us children for its carved legs and velvet seat cushions shining with shining polish and on this all of us including three of us brothers and two of our aunt's children. Used to sit around her and used to insist on telling the story. Aunt of innocent nature used to mix with us children and become a child. Today, like Rasool Chachi, that bed has also lost its charm."Why don't you tell me your name?"

Trying unsuccessfully to recognize her twinkling eyes, Rasoolan sat up and started fumbling for her spectacles on her bed, when Alok Babu held out the spectacles near the pillow and quickly caught hold of them."Babua! I don't recognize you." "I am Munna Chachi! Avadharai's youngest son." "Hey Munna! how many years have passed since you child and your father left here."

Chachi was looking at Munna with great curiosity that the happiness on her face suddenly turned into sadness. Cleaning the fogged glasses of her glasses she said, "Brother, now everything is desolate and lost. Chhuttan and Qasim had paased away. I Marjani am sitting with a stone on my chest to recite Fatiha. Everything lost after going you. Riots happened and the witch ate everything. Brother! the relationship, the responsibility of brotherhood, everything took with them. Both the Britons fell victim to all person's ferocity in the same riot.

Chachi continued to speak non-stop as if the slag of canker that had been buried for years wanted to come out to get relief from its pain and Alok Babu's facial expressions were changing color with each passing breath.

Unseen fear was starting to appear in the eyes that were stuck to the palate like a tongue. The garden of sweet memories like the beautiful mulberry of childhood has turned into a haunted forest of acacia. Fear began to haunt that aunt's hand-made straw hats and bags for Babuji and tobacco with golden knotted stars started burning in front of the eyes like sparks of flint.

Alok Babu was being suppressed by unwanted guilt that he kept asking,"Aunt, are you not angry with me?" "No, Bitwa!" Alok Babu got some satisfaction. Now it seems that even if something has changed, not everything has changed.

The raw living in the corner of the courtyard was the same, only the stairs had become small due to wear and tear. Going down to the courtyard of our house through the roof was a good pastime for all of us children to entertain ourselves. But now it seemed that somewhere the roof's path was lost. The well in the courtyard was as deep as it was but the water had become cloudy as if moss had mixed in the water of the Ganges and the water had become muddy.

A silence was starting to dissolve in the darkness of the evening. Alok Babu's mind was getting trapped in the whirlpool of sadness. The neighbor's aunt, whom he had seen making small betel leaves out of her glittering pandan, feeding all children with great love, today she opened the same black rustied pandan, it is not known what she was looking for in it, if she want to open the pandan and heal the taste of her mouth with the memories buried in it.

Aunt broke the silence and said, "And Babua! how are you all at home?" "Mother and Babuji are no more, the rest two brothers are busy with their jobs and home. I have come to Hardoi a few days ago after being transferred. There is only your bride in the house, there is no child of her."Seeing Alok Babu's eyes lying on the kitchen in the corner. It seemed that the stove was stayed cold today."Have you eaten anything, aunty?" Alok Babu started repenting after asking such an arrogant question."Yes, Hamida Baji' son will come with chapatis and salan in a while. By the grace of Allah, he is the one who takes care of me now."

Alok Babu was looking at Rasoolan very carefully. The fair hands in which bangles kept tinkling, those hands were made of bamboo splinters. When aunt used to walk, she used to wave her braided hairless cover and the gust of wind smelling of perfume would touch all of us and go away. Alok Babu was thinking today that what was so special in the eyes of the aunt and in her words that all of us brothers used to hang around her. If we put our hands on her betel leaf, she would have understood that we needed betel leaves, even if we had to be scolded by Amma Babuji, but we were so sure that we would cross the roof and wall of this house and our house ten times a day. And eating betel leaves made by our aunt had become our daily bread and pulses.

"Where are you staying now, Munna?" "I stayed in the government office." "Will you stay now or not?" "I will leave tomorrow itself, since I am on official duty"Meanwhile, aunt got up and went to the closet adjacent to the vestibule and brought a knotted bag and pliers. While biting betel nut with pliers, two drops of tears fell from behind the spectacles, which she wiped with her cover. She said while increasing the paan, "Take this Babuaa! Another things are not having us. What will I give to eat?"

Alok Babu's hands were trembling while holding the paan. Which eye that was buried in the ground of relationship became alive by raising its head that Alok Babu got up even against his will."Let I go aunty, I will come again" Since the aunt could not believe, hence she asked again, "Tell me, again when will you come? Khuda Hafiz" "Yes, yes, I will definitely come. Khuda Hafiz, aunty!" Alok Rai came out pushing the door with his heavy heart.

*****